Fog & Car was designed by
Bookmobile Design & Digital Publisher Services.
Text is set in Source Serif Pro.

Photo © Ning Li

EUGENE LIM is the author of the novels *The Strangers* (Black Square Editions, 2013; reissue forthcoming from Coffee House Press, 2026), *Dear Cyborgs* (FSG Originals, 2017), and *Search History* (Coffee House Press, 2022). His writings have appeared in *The Brooklyn Rail, The Baffler, Dazed, Fence, Little Star, Granta,* and elsewhere. He is a high school librarian, runs Ellipsis Press, and lives in Queens, New York, with Joanna and Felix.

Praise for *Search History*

***Literary Hub,* "Most Anticipated Books of 2021"**

***The Millions,* "Most Anticipated of 2021"**

***Bustle,* "Best Books of October 2021"**

"Fans of Haruki Murakami's melancholy, oneiric tales will also delight in Lim's assault upon consensus reality. He encourages the reader to 'stop making sense,' in the Talking Heads manner, and experience the universe as a magical tapestry of events whose overall pattern is perceivable only by God—or maybe after one's own death."

—Paul Di Filippo, *The Washington Post*

"Sometimes new works arrive, such as Eugene Lim's strange, sinuous, highly memorable novel *Search History* that seem to herald some dawning technological epoch. . . . A work of eerie and lasting power."

—Sam Sacks, *The Wall Street Journal*

"[A] humorous philosophical novel, which entertains questions about the nature of narrative and the aesthetic implications of technology. Subversions of the conventional structure of the novel abound. . . . As the book toggles between the narrator's autobiography, a meandering quest for the friend, and conversations among the search party about grief, selfhood, and Asian American authorship, Lim evokes the disorienting idiosyncrasy of an Internet search history." ***—The New Yorker***

"A post-human manifesto on loss, identity, and the transfigurative potential of art. . . . This brilliant sui generis takes storytelling to new heights." ***—Publishers Weekly,* starred review**

"As befits a book dealing with death and rebirth, the novel oscillates between the uncanny and the philosophical. . . . Lim brings together the mundane and the extraordinary to powerful effect."

***—Kirkus,* starred review**

"This novel is very funny. It has a quick wit that comes on barrel-chested, deriding at times poetry, the neo-liberal consensus, and various pop culture ephemera. . . . *Search History* is a living, breathing novel. Its fascinations and enthusiasms are important yet ambivalent. . . . Mature, without being self-serious or fatalistic. An *Ode to Joy* in Autotune." **—Joseph Houlihan, *Chicago Review of Books***

Praise for *Dear Cyborgs*
***BOMB Magazine,* "Best of 2017"**
***Vol. 1 Brooklyn,* "Favorite Fiction Books of 2017"**
***Chicago Review of Books,* "Best Books of 2017"**
***The Millions,* "Most Anticipated"**
***Literary Hub,* "Favorite Books of 2017"**

"Transfixing from page to page, filled with digressive meditations on small talk and social protest, superheroes, terrorism, the art world, and the status of being marginal. . . . There's an intoxicating, whimsical energy on every page. Everything from radical art to political protest gets absorbed into the rhythms of everyday life."

—Hua Hsu, *The New Yorker*

"A novel about art and resistance, and how they may spur each other on, or frustrate their respective goals. In structure it resembles the great mid-century metafictions. . . . Eugene Lim's super-comrades, with their cultural disaffection and nuanced political opinions, offer a rather more compelling version of a collective consciousness."

—David Hobbs, *Times Literary Supplement*

"Two radically different story lines are cleverly tied together in this short, sly, unorthodox novel. . . . The core relationships, whether they're between estranged childhood friends or opinionated superhumans, are real and profoundly moving." **—*Publishers Weekly,* starred review**

"A novel of ideas, small, elegant ideas about art and protest, and one of the most striking literary works to emerge from the Occupy movement. . . . I had expected the decade's wave of protests to yield a raft of conventional social novels—some earnest, some satirical, perhaps not a few reactionary—but in *Dear Cyborgs* Lim has delivered something far more idiosyncratic, intricate, and useful: a novel that resists and subverts conventions at every turn." **—Christian Lorentzen, *New York Magazine***

"I know I'm reading a good book when it makes me mutter, What is this? Eugene Lim's slim and very weird *Dear Cyborgs* evoked that response in me plenty of times. . . . *Dear Cyborgs* is like the image inside a kaleidoscope, especially if that image comes from the midnineties cyberpunk-tinged dream of a middle-aged vegan asleep in Zuccotti Park circa 2011. In other words: it certainly keeps you on your toes."

—Jeffery Gleaves, *The Paris Review*

FOG & CAR

ALSO BY EUGENE LIM,
FROM COFFEE HOUSE PRESS

Search History
The Strangers (forthcoming, 2026)

FOG & CAR

⦿ ⦿ ⦿

EUGENE LIM

WITH AN INTRODUCTION BY
Renee Gladman

COFFEE HOUSE PRESS
Minneapolis
2024

First published in 2008 as *Fog & Car* by Ellipsis Press

Cover design by Michael Salu

Coffee House Press books are available to the trade through our primary distributor, Consortium Book Sales & Distribution, cbsd.com or (800) 283-3572. For personal orders, catalogs, or other information, write to info@coffeehousepress.org.

Coffee House Press is a nonprofit literary publishing house. Support from private foundations, corporate giving programs, government programs, and generous individuals helps make the publication of our books possible. We gratefully acknowledge their support in detail in the back of this book.

LIBRARY OF CONGRESS CATALOGING-IN-PUBLICATION DATA

Names: Lim, Eugene, author.
Title: Fog & Car / Eugene Lim.
Other titles: Fog and Car
Description: Minneapolis : Coffee House Press, 2024.
Identifiers: LCCN 2023059226 (print) | LCCN 2023059227 (ebook) | ISBN 9781566896931 (paperback) | ISBN 9781566896948 (epub)
Subjects: LCGFT: Novels.
Classification: LCC PS3612.I46 F64 2024 (print) | LCC PS3612.I46 (ebook) | DDC 813/.6—dc23/eng/20240117
LC record available at https://lccn.loc.gov/2023059226
LC ebook record available at https://lccn.loc.gov/2023059227

PRINTED IN CANADA

31 30 29 28 27 26 25 24   1 2 3 4 5 6 7 8

TO MY FATHER KUN BOO LIM
TO MY MOTHER KEUN HEE LIM
TO MY SISTER KAREN PARK LIM

Introduction

I returned to Eugene Lim's *Fog & Car,* fifteen years after it was first published, with the wrong mindset. I'd been thinking, "Oh cool. I can treat this introduction like a reunion with old friends," characters I hadn't encountered since 2008, whom I didn't remember exactly but whose shapes spun perpetually in a corner of my mind. I tried to recall the blurb I'd written for the book, hoping that would provide a flood of information about who Fog and Car were, so that when we re-met, it would be with a productive familiarity. All I could bring up from the vault of fragments that sometimes performs as my memory was a sense that I'd written about many people sort of crowded together; maybe I'd talked about noise or overlapping connections. Ultimately, recall was not achieved, and I had to hunt down the actual blurb in the real world. This is what I found:

> The events of this novel take place in a space contrary to action, illuminating the silences of the page and the nothing that haunts the borders of "doing something." A beautifully paced and thoughtful work.

And had to recalibrate my approach. Once I immersed myself in this novel, for the second time, fifteen years older, post so many traumatic and outrageous events having occurred in the world, on both domestic and international levels, at scales miniscule and gargantuan, I understood that the long-standing impact of this novel had less to do with an affinity for the characters as much as it did with the uniquely intimate and unsettling way Lim reveals the precarity of their aloneness. "We are, each of us, alone" is a quote that gets thrown about, although I can't determine who said it first. I was sure it was Virginia Woolf's Mr. Ramsay, but his thoughts are, "We perished, each alone," himself quoting a famous poem and being a bit more fatalist than is warranted here. But it is true: we are on our own, in our bodies and minds. And what's worse (and rendered exquisitely in this novel) is that our shape or solidity as a person is determined by how our language flows, how it listens to us, and what it does to our form when there isn't anyone necessarily on the other side—at the end of a sentence or thought—to receive us. Lim puts it best, in a moment of indirect self-reflection by one of the titular characters: "Perhaps in his imaginings, in his mental talking and drawing of various shapes and constructions to describe his problem, he is creating not models and maps but other problems, and so, stepping back to see his progress, realizes all his efforts are simply increasing the empty space that the answers would, had there been any, occupy."

In this novel, Lim slows down interior time by flooding the narrative with tasks, by placing those tasks in a syntax that's just slightly off cue, exemplified by these two moments from different places within the story: "He finally admits his stupor. Soap in the cabinet, opens a bar of it. The green paper thrown, a flight of soap" and "She closed the door, retracted her leg, and then for several moments did not move at all." These ordinary actions take on an almost grotesque quality, something "extra" but also funny—absurd, elongated nearly beyond recognition, twisted toward progress. For Fog and Car, a recently divorced couple, re-establishing themselves as single people separated by a few states, stumbling into and through new desires, grabbing a drink from the refrigerator, moving into a new apartment, making plans, looking out the window become labyrinthine in what they propose, in what they promise for each character's sense of subjectivity.

So, I correct myself: it's less that events are taking place "contrary to action" than that the environment in which those events occur is vast, deserted, and without company: "He was there and she here, living each with the ebb and flow of the other's ghost."

Then company comes.

But company doesn't bring relief exactly, and that has to do with the problem of progress, which, as evidenced by Lim's extraordinary syntactical constructions, is more than a pushing forward, a line cutting through. It may not be in front of us at all. However, Fog and Car want to progress. They want to succeed, to heal, to bring things to a close then move on; and, just like the rest of us, they were taught that to succeed you must *do.* You must grab yourself and go, even our language makes us behave in this way, with no way to reverse course, detour, make a new line perhaps perpendicular to the one we're on, make a line full of ellipses.

For me, this time through this novel, I feel a strong longing for things to stop moving entirely. For Fog and Car to stop wanting, to stop following, to stop seeking consequences, to stop drinking, to stop fucking. One major thing this novel asks but sensibly fears the answer to is what happens after.

What takes the place of spinning and forward motion and completing tasks? What is a novel of nothing, of open, of clear?

This is not that novel but is something made of what would beckon it; emptying as it floods and flooding as it empties.

Renee Gladman
August 2023

On the highway they began to encounter the fog. It seemed in the rush of the car to come and meet them. It came suddenly, with a rush and in a moment nothing could be seen but the white billows of water crossed in front by the flares of the headlights.

—William Carlos Williams
from *The Great American Novel*

A problematic sense of self-respect. Something lost in trying to kick against the pricks unless the vision, call it, is complete, and secures itself in its own inviolability. Blake says, I am Socrates. John said that in the act of non-adaptation to the demands of an economic system may lie a commitment to the system's forms far more destructive an involvement than any simple-minded conformity. But such a long and dull sentence it had to seem.

—Robert Creeley
from *The Island*

FOG & CAR

PART ONE MIRROR

Mr. Fog

THEY HAVE COME, early, to a river without a bridge. Scuttle down the sides the papers fly from their pockets in the race to a cool water. The banks are muddy but one of them has swum here before, come through the woods. That one says he would take him to a small fort on an island deep in the woods where, did he know? there's a river. He didn't know and the creek's ravine is satisfying and secret.

He has come here in a dream though that is a mistake, it happening before so it is a memory but so fuzzed as to make the friend this or that one perhaps not him or him and the creek is a river is a small lake never big and always hidden in thickets or groves and always a wood deep and delicious in the size of memory (though the road was not far).

A certain memory then, of objects that substantiate his movements, these memories this nostalgia incorporates into this doing of this exact moment. It is this drumsong and this engraving on a leather belt, this hat, and this ravine.

After his divorce, he moves to Ohio, a small town. Now it is late August in a mild summer. September will begin soon, so will the cool season and boys come to the field, play soccer while the light remains.

The lake. Several days will pass there. In his bag, several sheets of paper. Each day in late summer in dead calm but in evening sun, he folds a boat. Blank pages all, each a letter. The drum marches distantly.

The accord set for whatever peace from battle. He imagines brightly clothed soldiers, a nineteenth-century war, thick and stiff clothing. Fields of battle shift and the paper boats can be let go in swift if not precise formation. Ringing the football field, the band's march. Time passes.

Say this: was there some moment past in a rosebush he as a small child small enough to travel in and under this bush and meet with a boy, this among secrets.

Now, sitting at the lake, he thinks about what he has done. One month before school begins where he has been hired as a teacher. He has moved to a house. His savings are ample, there is a smelly part of town. He rents an entire house there.

He remembers also someone older on a celebratory day on a hill poke holes in a tin can and place blue hot coals inside, whirling it round on a string and whooping whooping circled by light. He once played in a ravine. Someone once gave him a hat; he speaks this language and knows these words in another and these in another and he writes with this one so he knows at least that he hears himself repeating tin can poked with holes tin can poked with holes tin can tin can tincan tincan tincan tincan tincan almost gone tincantincantincantincan almost gone but turning away from it, eyes closed to feel the wind off the lake, he finds laughing that there it is ready to bite again, tin can.

So he, beside the lake, with a preoccupation, admittedly childish, of paper boats. He recognizes that he is purposely creating drama and its accompanying landscape to relieve. The picture wakes him to the relevant fact. He has recreated, no—re-envisioned, heroically—a child playing alone. As the thought finishes, the theater lights fade and he is again beside the lake.

HE FEELS A PANIC as he thinks about his new job. As he eases out of it. She would have approved. A productive waiting she would have called it.

His wife. The words beat twice, are the snares of the marching band. Da dum, da dum, da dum.

She sends him letters, their envelopes containing blank pages. He has been thinking about her.

And the other? Which one was it. Oh yes the dear friend. Who came and we sang, what did we sing. Was it that one. Oh yes it was him. Oh yes the dear friend. When we sang. Which one. And the song. Which.

It must have been his birthday. You had arranged a party for he was your friend and it was his birthday. But they left the crowd because you and he could set up a rosebush, large and filling out the street with a strong flush of alcohol and there was the sun, not set, and a spring day and there was talk. So with thoughts, you think, there is not this man or that but him once. Even now you can summon the warm face, the blood thick in the face from the drinking, your forehead and his meet and a shout throated and released. The stone walls and bricks of the street clear and empty, a chamber for his voice for his cry of life. Oh deep sound. Put your hand to your face, his forehead once there, so it is, you confess, not this, that, but this, and that is memory, fear living there.

There is the event of them in several habits of conversation. At his house or his house, at the restaurant, at the bar. And the memory arises of those (that) occasions (occasion): Communion Communication Fraternity. The words sway in his mind and as he forces the remembering, he thinks those Historian words, smoothing fact into theory. When it was the two of them, sitting, discrete.

SCHOOL BEGINS but he is not there, asleep in front of the class, a voice settling on the shelves and heads, an addition to the room's dust and light. A friend whom he saw in the past. For a while, daily.

HE IS THE GREEDY HORSE starving between two bags of oats, choosing between paradoxes, mind faltering to know if one empty, the other wise. In his brain, the friend and his wife, standing equally on two opposing lobes, asking of him.

After school he walks past the lake to his home. There is a letter in the mailbox, another letter from his wife—his ex-wife—so she is still there, she has found him and is living somewhere new again, so he takes the time to reply, thinking maybe then he can rise from his chair.

It is only an accident, however, and the chair fits just as well. He knows the sadness of the unraveling, which, not bitter, after all, begun some years ago, but still the unraveling shows like the dust on the mirror shelf. What to do with it, too gone for repair though repair is cheap in every purchase save the doing.

THE CHILDREN ASK HIM questions; it is difficult for him to respond. Somehow the unlawed, the criminals of James A. Garfield Public High School, act with mercy in the classroom of what everyone knows, adult and child alike, to be an imitation.

Criminals of a type, flush they both had been in the face, when they found the briar patch, a thorny young creature and not thick but thick enough for the hiding of them, had arisen in a lot they had never seen. Examining it, they went under, the other leading, tearing at the ground with their fingers hoping to get to the center. It was there that they did and hid their criminal acts: he had taken a bottle of his father's whiskey there, so their drinking partnership was early established, and he had brought cheese and bread.

They started early on a Saturday and were sick by ten in the morning. They dug holes in the earth for their vomit and were scared of dying and whipping both so sat there eating the cheese sandwiches. Their minds were soft and liquid, the branches netted the sky above them, he thought he wouldn't mind the dying and someday he might bring a girl here and do the same and perhaps that was what love was and sobering by evening went home to a scolding, of course, triumphant.

Was it him, truly, had they traveled away together, to the city together, or was it a semblance of him that he had later met in the city and put the two together as they served the same purpose. This man or that woman, accidents and coincidence were the substance of his memories so what could those words possibly mean? That his dreams had objects which he juggled and slapping these objects into his palm and hurling them without caution into the air, and he sat in his chair studying at a distance the picture of this violent juggler and watched the violence below nonetheless spring into perfect arcs of motion above, listless sitting watching.

And when he had gone away to another city, finally to another language and another country, how he had met his wife. And she was a coincidence also, yet he thought that their combat fit his ideas of marriage. They had stood outside a restaurant in Tierra del Fuego and shivered and they had both turned, he from an old way that he had forgotten, and she in some—wonderful he had thought at the time—auguring of his action, and each pantomimed the other so that they both turned and plugged a nostril with a finger and voided mucus onto the snow. He stood facing her and behind them both, two snot blobs in the snow.

In San Francisco, he is in a hotel bed with his wife. He thinks that he is hungry, as they had traveled the whole day to get here and only had one cup of coffee, too excited or busy to have eaten. Well, the truth is that circumstances had mismanaged his stomach. They had gotten up, had the cup of coffee and there met the man who was going to Las Vegas, half the way, right that moment. So off they went and the same happened in Las Vegas so now here they were, she tired and happy, he anxious and hungry and happy.

Preparing for bed, a partial light from the street lamp. The window open, the room is filled with a coolness. His clothes are not twisted and his sheets are straight. He is wearing cotton sweat pants and a T-shirt and his mind is blank.

HE HAS RETURNED. An evening in fall he searches through a wood and finds a river, now with a bridge. He carefully walks down the embankment, making sure nothing in his pockets comes unburied and stands at the creek.

He feels conscious of taking the time after his divorce, the sadness, picking that up like a roll of dough and stretching it. He knows he does so with a penitent's selfishness, the infirm pleasure that came after the heart broke, reviewing the breaking.

Then after a while, it isn't even the breaking, but the sound of the action that he follows out, rode upon to seek other similarities.

GOING TO SLEEP HE notices the lamplight of this room is almost the exact color of this other lamplight in this other room, and he sickens with sadness and desire to go to this other room with this other light. In his dreams he goes there to find it is the same room and wishes to wake to regain the former but it is by then day and the light and wall, so inconsistent their ellipse of movement and so precise his memory of color, never repeat.

Ms. Car

A FEW WEEKS AFTER CAR DIVORCED her husband, she found a one-bedroom apartment. She had taken her belongings to her mother's and was there now sorting out boxes of kitchen-ware and clothes.

You should leave your books and records here, her mother had said, until you think the place is permanent.

Huh, why? Who knows how long you'll live there and then you'll have to lug all this stuff all over again. But Mom, I want the stuff there so it'll *feel* permanent. But you don't know, it could get robbed . . . all the bad stuff happens in the beginning before you're settled. I'll be alright.

Oh fine, do what you want, her mother said as she moved to the window. You sure you can drive that? She motioned to the large yellow van that was parked in the driveway.

I'm sure. It's a nice van though, isn't it? That! it's an eye-sore. Mother, it isn't.

She considered its dented rust, came to the same conclusion, but kept silent. After a while she said, Well, be careful. Driving a van isn't the same as driving a car.

The mother went back to the kitchen, smiling. Car was tired from packing but would not stop as she wanted to leave immediately after lunch. She also feared sitting still would allow her to mourn, which she was tired of doing. She so busied herself with packing books and folding dishes into towels and newspaper that when her mother called to say that lunch was ready she was finishing, and looking for a place to put the scissors and tape.

Who's going to eat all this? The small kitchen table was loaded with food—sandwiches, potato salad, a pitcher of iced tea, and a store-bought cake. Her mother told her to hurry if she wanted to leave in time. Packing had made her hungry and she followed her mother's orders.

Is that everything you need? Yes, I think so. OK, well take care and drive safe. I will, Mom, thank you. Take care of yourself. Bye! Bye!

It was late afternoon by the time she made the highway. The sun was low and the sky clear and she felt happy to be driving. She was grateful to her mother for acting simply and trying to spoil her. In spite of what she had said, she was scared to drive the large van in the city. But soon she was fighting the weekend traffic, feeling like she was returning to a familiar game, one that she had missed. She honked her horn generously and felt like each mile was bringing her closer into the city's heat and noise. When she got to the bridge, she felt it was too bad that she had to pay attention to the road and couldn't watch the view as it panned by, but soon she was in the thick of the city and her thoughts were attuned only to driving.

She parked the borrowed van near her new apartment and called the friend who had said she would help her unpack. She began taking a few boxes up to her new apartment. The rooms, empty of furniture, looked still small, and she was thankful she hadn't many belongings to clutter the space. She surveyed the rooms that looked as if they had been quickly and cosmetically cleaned, and not recently either, so she filled a bucket with soap and water and began to clean off the grime from the floors and walls.

I wonder if I should go down and wait for them or if they'll come up and find me, haven't even tested the buzzer yet, hope it works . . . And at that moment, as if in answer, the metallic disruption sounded.

Hello? Hallo Car, it's Sonya, buzz us in. Wait, I'll be down . . . And she quickly went down the flights to the street.

Hey, you don't have that much stuff, good. Yes, I was packing light. Her friend's boyfriend looked into the van and said, Do you have any furniture other than that love seat? No, though there's a mattress underneath all those boxes. Alright then, uhp!, here we go. Is the door unlocked? No, I'll have to go up with you. I'll wait by the van. Wait, let me get the door.

They spent the next half hour marching up and down the stairs. They chatted very little, trying to keep up their momentum. Car had packed the boxes densely and they were heavy. She really didn't have that many things, however, and soon the large van had been emptied.

Fearing the stores would close, she went out to buy a mop and cleaning supplies before it got too late. She spent the greater part of the evening unpacking the boxes and arranging her things. Finally, already after midnight, she wiped and scrubbed the kitchen and bathroom, mopped the floors, and took a quick, pleasant shower. She crawled into the sleeping bag, which she had unrolled on top of her mattress, and immediately fell asleep.

SHE WOKE UP LATE AND SOON was in the kitchen, chopping vegetables. She had invited a few people over for dinner, and it was the first time in a long time that she had thrown a party. She invited Sonya and Dan. It had in fact been Sonya who had proposed she have a housewarming party, and also promised to bring a few other people. It was into fall now and she was thinking of cooking a fat, festive dinner. Not knowing how exactly to do this, she had shopped generally. She chopped onions carelessly, and in her mind made up and discarded possible dishes.

She was still getting familiar with her new kitchen, which was small but clean. The floor was broken in the corner and the rooms needed a new paint job, but she noted these deficiencies only as future repairs. Soon she had meat roasting in the oven and several potlids on the stovetop, rattling with boil. The kitchen's window was white with steam and she took off her sweater and wiped her hands on her pants in satisfaction. Her pace was relaxed. Every so often she went into the other room, opened the window to let some of the heat out. She stood in front of the window and smoked a cigarette and sipped from a can of beer. Even with the window open, the apartment felt warm and she wished she could take a nap, but she thought she might oversleep and also had to watch the oven. The day passed quickly and soon it was time for the guests to arrive.

Sonya arrived with Dan and another man in tow, named Yasha. Good to meet you, he said, and Car disliked him quickly. There was another buzz and Sonya said that it might be her friend Hamish, whom she also had invited. Car ushered the new arrivals in and sat them down at a card table she had dressed for dinner.

So how do you know Sonya and Dan? Yasha asked.

We met in college. Sonya and I were roommates. How do you know them?

Both Hamish and I work with Sonya at the magazine.

What do you do there? Hamish's a fact-checker and I write a sports column.

Car shifted in her seat and said, Sounds good.

Not a big sports fan? Why do you say? Oh, I can tell.

Are you from New York? Hamish asked. Nope, I was living before this in Chicago with my ex.

Ah.

And now I'm here. What do you do? Right now, I have a job that Dan actually got me tending bar. My friend, you know him, Hamish, who owns McAleer's. Oh yeah, you're working there? Yep, I'll pour you a drink sometime. Hamish laughed, great.

Car went up to turn on some music and brought a bottle of wine back to the table. Here you go, she said, filling up the glasses. And a toast to Dan who helped me find a job when I needed it. To Dan! they toasted.

Chicago's great, said Yasha.

Yes it is.

It's a real city.

You've lived there? Car asked without interest.

Yes, I actually worked for a paper there a couple of years ago.

She abruptly went to the kitchen and brought back some whiskey.

Do you want some of this?

Yasha said, Oh, you've read my mind.

Ignoring him, she made herself a drink and placed the bottle on the table.

IT WAS DAN'S BIRTHDAY PARTY and she could hear music and a cloud of voices as she approached from the street. She was slightly timid, but the door opened immediately and someone already tipsy said, Come In! Come In! She put her coat on a bed and glanced around for a familiar face. None being found, she walked toward the liquor.

She poured herself a drink and relaxed. She asked someone for a cigarette.

It isn't any of his business. Well he got her out of it. They were both in a jam. We're doing location scouting. You're a lucky man. Maybe grad school? Har har! Oh, don't be such a dick. Carol's working at a new magazine. No fucking way! You wanna smoke out on the balcony? What kind of magazine? God that's a nice body. What were you doing in Texas?

Have you seen Sonya? Car asked. I think she's on the balcony, the voice added, with Dan.

She pulled back the screen door and stepped out into the night air. Hello! How's your new job? Not so bad, it's an easy bar, not so many rowdies. I like rowdies! Sure you do. You should stop by. Will you give us free drinks? Sure. Great. This is a nice place. Yeah but it's a long commute. At least you've got some space and this, even a view. It isn't much of one. Still.

Car's throat was dry. She had finished her drink and wasn't sure if it was too soon to leave the balcony. Sonya rescued her by saying, let's go in, it's too cold out here. She followed them but split off to get another drink.

Well, give me your number and I'll call you with his. Put on some different music! The guy was, you know, pissed, but he didn't know he, no, the other guy, had a crowbar hidden in his, yeah, and yeah, coked up. Yes, I'll call. And he beat the shit out of him, in the subway car. Then why do you come to them? A weekly glossy. For a New Jersey paper. You could take him home with you. No, he lived, thank god or, no, actually it all matters on which judge, on which judge. Fact-checking. I'm a bartender. You kind of look like one. It all depends on which judge he gets. What's a bartender look like? Aloof.

Car saw a space on the couch and debated whether to sit down. She felt better with the glass in her hand, and though the room was too noisy to hear the clink, it was a comfort to feel the ice knock against the glass.

DAN SHOWED UP AT THE BAR like he had said he would. She poured him drinks and talked to him in between customers.

I have a confession to make, she said. What's that? I think I'm going to quit this job. Why? I don't like it. Fair enough. It was nice of you to get it for me. Don't mention it. But thanks.

OK, Car. But you've only worked this job for two months.

It's enough time.

I suppose it is.

Are you mad?

Why would I be?

You went to the trouble.

Don't give it another thought. What are you going to do?

I'm going to try to get a job doing some proofreading. I have some leads.

Alright.

Dan left and she had a drink of her own to celebrate. Nor did she stop. She felt self-conscious drinking where she worked and at closing time went out to search for another bar. Tonight, I'm out to annihilate myself, she thought.

Mr. Fog

PERHAPS IT WAS BECAUSE the incident of his conception was the only thing he could remember his mother telling him about his origin and then even then he wouldn't hear her voice in the story but, blurring how he dreamt with what he dreamt, the imagery conflated, and he would see merely the fragments to some old film, reeling continually in a corner of his memory and to which he, pausing from the actual activity of the moment, would lift up his head, gaze toward, and catch a glimpse of. And now he reconstructs the details given to him from that sad, wasted woman whom he loves because she could forget herself for the fates of celluloid subway riders.

Preparing for bed, a partial light from the streetlamp. The window open, the room is filled with a coolness. His clothes are not twisted and his sheets are straight.

Movie houses and not the lonely sensual magic that reigned from them would leave him breathless and panting. With lights dimming, he would feel, regardless of the picture, the vacuum of disappointment coupled with the mutual satiation and disgust of overeating. Fog did not even associate this feeling with movie houses until one night after sex as he was falling asleep he spoke: I've seen it already.

Now, he is falling asleep, thinking about him and her and her, him, the people flashing through his mind, enduring somehow in the crevices to make appearance in both pure and conglomerate forms, habitats precise and multiple. He dreams. *She*

sat with a flirtatious smile that was actually hard and flat on a barstool in South Korea and

blind drunk

the man in fatigues slurred

Ahn ya hah say oh, how much?

Thirty-one and getting too old for the army base, even the dingier dives, and even the more drunken Americans, from a small southern village, she

And there was the other voice also, other voices, breaking in. There were the two losses, and it was possible that it was always a loss, a perpetual singular direction, and he had begun losing the friend when he had first made Ohio. He had remained in his desk, sweating, after school.

He was a Texan, a grocer's son

Her parents were long dead. And then they met in a bar.

He ended taking her to a movie house, an action-adventure. They sat in the dark last row.

It was the choice of distances to the door that was making him sweat. This is Zeno first done in a classroom or after class talking to the friend or perhaps it is at the briar or in the rosebush they have made, the friend explaining over and over, go halfway to the door then halfway then halfway halfway. Start over.

She placed a hand on his leg, understanding

A voice on screen saying, The mind of such . . . the intelligence of it . . . going to evil.

Fucking on the movie house floor.

A shot of brown shoes, seen earlier. They identify the villain without giving him an identity. Also: black leather gloves using electrician's tape to place a bomb on the tracks of a subway.

He was done so he got up to get a drink he said.

Handsome the hero dashes

Leaves

down the stairs of the subway station, knowing the certainty of his mission, gleaming in his duty and sweaty effort to do the world good. She sits up and watches to the end of the picture.

Fog takes her out of the movie theater knowing she knows and has her go out to a soda shop for a Coke. Later she would pick up one last soldier who would take her, him inside, to Ohio.

And that was as far as he could do it, not giving her a story around the single moment or choice in any decision, for the movie went blank and the movie house lifted up her lights and blazed a blank white until they were in America and life began at six, the rest unlived unremembered and only the single scene made possible by that long-lost voice of pictures that mesmerized him in his deepest sleep, a dance of light and film and voice, finally, voices, his friend seen at every age in the progression to loss, heard still, remembered, singing, also.

But the restaurant and the bar and your house

Subway station. Brown shoes. Electrician's tape.

and your house and his and his and the bed that we went to, for the sake of it, but it was this song that he read to me from that book and the leather belt with the engraving. That he gave? That he gave to him. And the hat that he

wore to meet his friend, was it in Chicago? at night near the last of their time together.

Similarly, he had been traveling with his wife, both of them across the country to San Francisco or possibly in the year that he had lived with his friend, lived together, that he mothered him, trying to talk a recovery.

There were the grooves, now beginning to show, the worn path of certain concerns.

The place where he slept was also an insistence. The return to it daily, the return to this town, made him think that as a child the fever that accompanied learning about paradoxes was, finally, the true instinct, returned to, also.

The song, then, which, bring it, it must have been, the *must* growing forceful not by confidence now but by a faith which was finally ascended to, like a religion, in powerlessness, so brought on, bring, the song they sang, once, or perhaps, the carelessness of his or her note, knowing that the other knew the song knew how the key had been recorded and listened to, now resang with that knowledge but not insisted upon because of the familiarity of both song and friendship,

brought on, sung, which, when, the triumphant note only the penultimate—for when for which were still but once and when were so—so brought, so bring, this song that, in moment,

There was coldness too of the giving in, but that perhaps temporary or lingering or growing, yes, eventually, to overtake but that too, temporary, brought on, bring it, a chamber rosebush filled with talk at this or that house restaurant bar lake, in the head, finally singing.

Ms. Car

TONIGHT, I'M OUT TO ANNIHILATE MYSELF, she thought. She knew of another bar not too distant that was quiet and cheap. She entered the bar, which was bright with fluorescent lights and ugly with flat paint of unmatching and inappropriate yellows. She had hoped to be left alone but since her clothes and manner were young, eventually several men began to sidle up to her and make coherent enough gestures. She was uncomfortable there also, and decided to go home.

She stepped out onto the street. She walked a bit farther and saw a Christmas tree left on the sidewalk to be taken away. Next to the tree she saw a man. As she walked closer she saw that he was nibbling on the tree.

She passed him and as she did, he stopped eating and walked with her. Taste good? she asked.

Hmm?

The tree.

Oh yes! it was delicious.

She laughed and said, You're drunk.

A little, not too bad. So are you, the man added.

Why do you say?

Because you keep bumping into me. Oh . . . she tried to make her steps more even.

I'll buy you a drink? he asked. Where? Here.

They were in front of a corner deli and there bought three cans of beer and then sat on a cement step, drinking.

She ventured, I'm working at this bar. I'll be working there for about two more weeks. You should stop by and I'll pay you back.

I'll do that.

They opened and split their odd beer. Happy holidays! he said. Happy holidays!

The next morning she woke up several times. Finally she sat up and was very thirsty. She went to the kitchen and drank a few cups of water and put on a kettle to boil for coffee. She wanted a cigarette but thought she might have left her pack at the bar. She searched her coat and felt the box in the pocket, and—smiled. Now, prepared, she sat next to the kitchen window, feeling refreshed.

SHE NEEDED WORK AND HAD answered an ad for a secretary. The morning of her interview she woke up late. She turned on the hot water for a shower. She hung the one appropriate outfit she owned in the bathroom and hoped it would steam enough of the wrinkles out to look presentable. Quickly she put on some makeup, dressed, and left the house.

The morning rush hour affected her badly, and she arrived at the interview tired and cranky. In very few words she answered questions about her experience and then was hired for the following week. She decided to do all her unpleasant errands in one go, and so afterward went to the post office to mail some bills. There was a long line when she entered the post office. A woman with a child. The child looked away and lifted her toes in time to a song she hummed. A young couple holding hands. A man listening to music through headphones. Letters, packages, or yellow notices to pick up packages. A man beside her sighed loudly. It was her turn. She mailed her bills and bought stamps. She went to a few stores and bought shampoo and trash bags.

This left the laundry and grocery shopping. She decided to do the laundry first, carried it to her apartment, folded her clothes. Next, she bought the groceries and brought them into the house and immediately put the packages of foods away.

She took an orange into the living room. She sniffed it as she peeled it, and qualifying her day with its smell, said, Well, glad that's over with.

ONE SUNDAY SHE WOKE UP early to find a fresh snow had fallen. She decided to go take a walk in the park and dressed and left her apartment. As she came out of the building, the cold shocked her awake. It had been a heavy snowfall and she heard a truck salt the roads. When she made the park, however, the sounds were hushed. The sky was finishing off its pink and looked like it would turn cloudless. She wanted to sit but knew she would get cold and would want to return, so, lit a cigarette and kept walking.

She spied children running in the distance with a sled. As she approached they were taking turns lying in the snow. Wonder what that's about? By the time she had gotten close enough to see they were making snow angels, they'd tired of this and were knocking each other about, throwing snowballs. She stared down at the depressions they had made. A snowball flew through the air, close to her face. She stood momentarily, and imagined if it had hit her, smack in the face. Suddenly she feared being ridiculed by them and walked on.

Leaving the park, she decided to continue through the city. She stood there, on the corner, making up her mind where to go. Along the street, a few shopkeepers were opening, lifting up the metal fences that caged their store windows, flipping signs from CLOSED to OPEN, shoveling snow from their share of sidewalk. She smelled a bakery and thought she would have something, but looking around couldn't find it. God, that smells good, she thought, where could it be? It was right in front of her, after all. Anything fresh? she asked. Everything's fresh, the girl said, but what d'ya want? Are those glazed still warm. Yes. I'll take one and a milk.

She ate it in the store, staring out the window and getting sugar on her coat. She thought she would like to leave the city one future weekend. She could rent a car and drive somewhere, maybe upstate or Connecticut, maybe to Vermont. Who do I know in Vermont? she thought.

I DIDN'T THINK YOU'D want to be a bartender for long.

Oh it wasn't so bad . . . She was meeting Sonya for lunch. Yes, Sonya said, but it's crazy, I told Dan so, but you two were so excited.

Well I thought I'd give it a shot. What are you doing now? I'm freelancing, copyediting, technical writing, even some translating. Hey, that's not bad. Yeah, my friend in Chicago really came through for me. At the publisher where you worked before. Yes.

Well, you know what it was, laughed Sonya . . . Dan envisioned, I think, this hangout for his circle. A kind of club.

Yes, said Car, I got that feeling.

Dan wants to do right but he has his own ideas. He's young at heart.

Yes, I think you've got him down.

Well, I should, by now . . . Car, I've something to say. Sonya had been bubbling something inside since they had sat down and Car by this time had a hunch.

You're pregnant!

How did you know? You haven't been able to sit still since we got here.

Well, yeah! she was laughing, I am.

God. Is it . . . How do you feel?

Scared and happy. Dan is very happy, his feet aren't on the ground, but we're both scared to death too.

Good, that's probably just right. Then after a while Car swore again, God.

She looked up at Sonya who was smiling. She said, Congratulations!

Thanks, said Sonya, and burst out laughing.

IT WAS A WEEKDAY AND SHE bought a paper and went to the closest theater for the show at the soonest time. She had been stuffed in her apartment for two days and had begun to be hungry for visuals, the differing brightnesses of the city. She was happy with her choice. The theater was dusty and from the walls hung dirty red curtains. The picture came on the screen with the overwhelming brightness of summer, the colors intensified by absence. The film's hero moved around obstacles with deftness, fought others with a staged but convincing action. She was taken with the movement of the film, quick, breathless, forcing her judgment to be taken over by instinct.

She left the theater to be surprised by daylight. Returning to her apartment, there was a beam of sun on her desk and her familiar papers were crisp white squares, bouncing this light onto the walls.

After that first trip to the movies, she made it a habitual break and usually saw a film every one or two weeks. She was a democratic moviegoer, choosing as she had the first time, by whichever movie played at a convenient time. If she saw one she liked, however, she'd go see it half a dozen times, as long as it was still running. Her husband had been like that, she thought one day after she had seen a film for the fourth time, we both are happy to be in our ruts. They had talked about this often enough and they had even taken a pride in how stubbornly they had regulated their lives. It was a gentle fact, not really completely true; they reinforced it, a small conspiracy of self deceit—for they were as mad and chaotic as anyone they knew, would lose hours in various simple distractions—but she had enjoyed these conversations, regularly spaced, which shaped their thoughts about one another.

SHE DOES, IN FACT, find someone in Vermont but not until spring. Not a someone, finally, but a place. She had mentioned she had wanted to go out of the city one day to a friend at the company she was doing technical writing for. Then, a week later, the thought almost out of mind, the woman had called up and said she knew someone who had a house in Vermont. The owner would be glad for someone to make use of it. Car accepted. When she had left she felt sorry that it was overcast, but now, on the road, great sweeps of land were to her sides and the sky was a mismatch of dramatic blues. When she actually arrived at the small town where the house was, she looked with approval onto the clouds, which were full with rain.

The house was musty from disuse. She opened all the windows and the rain began, bringing with it the smell of wet grass. She had brought some groceries from town and was preparing to cook dinner. There was a television in the house and she turned it on, listened to a weatherman speak as she cooked.

After dinner she examined the owner's shelves and noticed a leftover collection of records, a strange variety of albums: a polka record, TV theme songs, a sound effects album, and records by Johnny Cash, Van Halen, and Ralph Stanley. She watched some more television and then poured herself a drink and listened to each record, carefully unsheathing each and wiping them with her sleeve before putting them away.

She put her drink down and stood up, danced for a while to some of the songs. She jumped around, dancing a polka—or what she thought might approximate a polka. She tapped a foot and smoked cigarettes to Johnny Cash. She listened curiously to the sound effects album; some were funny and silly, others were eerie to be heard without context, alone in the house. She decided to listen to Ralph Stanley and sat feeling herself distant from the city. Eventually she found some blankets and fell asleep on the couch.

The next morning she was impatient to drive home but had planned to spend a few days at least, so fought the urge. She took out her papers and began working. She actually had quite a bit of work to do, indexing an academic book and writing a few short articles for a pharmaceutical company. She sat and worked through the day, every once in a while getting up to put on a record.

Mr. Fog

THERE WERE TWO LOSSES he remembered. Two endings.

The friend who had grown increasingly angry. And his divorce.

The friend had proceeded to cut everyone off.

And it wasn't anger either. Which has a knife in it, but a kind of dying inside the friend, a blank weight smothering relentlessly.

He had tried to talk him out of it.

But it wasn't the right method in the end, somehow, but was the only one he knew.

He hadn't tried to talk his wife out of anything. He had said to her not to leave and then

after a while of that, kept silent.

He even moved in with him, for a year. Lived together in an apartment and like a parent stood over him

waiting, concerned.

He, the friend, answered all questions with null answers.

Do you want? I don't know.

Gradually he had lost contact with his friend, whom he had known for a long time.

They had grown up together, grown apart through different interests, grew back together over beers and buzzing talk.

He had been his best man and he his. The friend's marriage lasted a year; his had lasted seven.

It was amazing to him that he had lost contact with this friend.

He had met the friend in this town, the one he has returned to.

He knew that the friend had lived in Philadelphia, Hong Kong, Singapore, and Seattle, and that he practiced law. One night, he had spent a few hours trying to find him, talking to strangers with his name.

By then, he could be living anywhere and probably was, living anywhere. He knew where his wife lived.

She had moved to New York, sent him a letter. In fact, it wasn't a letter but she had inherited a tic from her father.

Her father was, all accounts seemed to confirm, genial and a loon.

He had visions of success, so, thought he should act on them, somehow lost interest when they neared him.

They had moved constantly when she was a girl, the father always on the hunt, chasing prospects.

Or so she had told him, late one night in her parents' home.

He tried to see it in the man whom he had met

who was smiling and infirm, a year away from death.

And so, upon moving, in order to keep in touch with his global array of chumps loafers and associates

her father would fold newly minted business cards into a white sheet of paper and mail these out.

Eventually the old man grew tired of this and just sent the white sheet of paper, the return address on the envelope

assuming that the recipient would think he forgot to put a card in.

And after a while it was just another of his pranks, and they loved him more for it.

So that now, he received, also, blank sheets of paper

and knew she had moved to New York.

Perhaps she sent these only to him, who knew the story

whom she had told it to.

For otherwise she kept silent.

Perhaps that was what his friend had done.

For habit after habit had gone. First the buzzing, then the talking, then even the drinking.

She had been protesting, actively protesting, when he had met her.

Living on nothing and doing nothing also

but there was a line, he could see, between the friend and his wife.

She lived on nothing and *did* nothing. Active.

While he simply sunk down.

Not a rebellion, finally, but a dying.

He wasn't sure to believe in that kind of distinction, come upon so. Maybe they were the same, finally.

Except not finally. She had answered his advertisement for Spanish lessons. That was how they had met.

In any case, she wasn't there doing the same thing; she was elsewhere doing something different.

The friend was elsewhere doing nothing different, he believed.

That kind of dying, much more consistent, nevertheless, than protest.

◉ ◉ ◉

CLEAR, EMPTY DAYS LIKE THIS, one after another,

he sits, lake in the periphery, glimpsed

through a breezy window, thinks to walk there

later. But now, he thinks to the table and the bag of oranges. On the table: old peels and seeds, letters, money, cigarettes, and his wife's letter. Did

he not respond, answer her, yesterday? He forgets, also asks himself, Are you hungry?

He can't remember if he ate his

breakfast,

often forgetting these days, then only remembering by the peels, orange seeds. He catches the lapse of his mind, usually does, by noon.

So what of it? he thinks, curious glance at the plate's rind

if I forget if I ate. Then wonders if it's time again to eat. He thinks this the better part of an hour before he sets his kettle to boil,

bringing it again to boil. Slicing some bread and cheese, he's done this nearly every Sunday this month, making it a ritual but doesn't realize it wholly.

His school schedule disrupting that, so he doesn't recognize his habit. He slaps a sandwich of rye bread, ketchup, some deli meat to fill it up, stands up to eat it. Why

bother? Lunch! His appetite is random, arbitrary, so he tries to keep a schedule or else he'll bloat. Or starve. The

thinking every day takes too long but he's powerless

to avoid it. Whistling just slightly, a happy smile, he echoes, "Are you hungry?" since he knows

how it is he works his mornings, rises, day after day, finally, sees it.

BROOM, WATER, PAIL—READY. He finally admits his stupor. Soap in the cabinet, opens a bar of it. The green paper thrown, a flight of soap

package to the trash. The rooms so dirty, all of them: in the kitchen, the refrigerator; bookshelves; bedrooms; the porch; mention the garage. Sweep

sideways and upstairs into the dustpan bin for hours. In fury, thinks: Have I always *meant* to do?

He takes a long time in the bathroom. Painful. Washing the sink and toilet, the bathtub—lingering before he scrubs it with Comet.

Doesn't this time think,

Why—if he did, never, he knows, would it get done—so always think this a burden?

before the rush of scrubbing stops.

Stretching again to help his waist and shoulders, back. He can't recall ever doing this as a repentance, also wishes wasn't doing it now. Pride

somehow. After that the trash must be prepared, the care that attends the paper, plastics. Damn foul thing he's in the sticks; neighbors will badger.

What for? them? the rat at the dumpster? their children? so he has to tie together the magazines.

Recycling takes too long but he does it with awe. To see the labor in systems

so layered and complexly displayed, asks again, *Haven't* I always meant to do? So he knows

what it is corrupts his doings, infiltrates his deeds, sinks him to armchair, lost in fog of memory, holds him.

WAS HE NOT THINKING about them anymore? But in fact, the light played in the background, and he was

remembering a day, St. Patrick's?—some holiday, maybe

yes, his friend's birthday, in March, some cobblestoned street in New York, in old SoHo, yes that was it, where they sat and sang a little song. That was a good memory from way back

it now seemed. He often confused it with a dusk or dawn in San Francisco—he couldn't remember—

a cross-country trip with his wife.

Perhaps it was the lighting that seemed so similar, the street where they had sung seemed enclosed, a chamber of white sunlight.

And the hotel in San Francisco, on Valencia Street, that too had been sundrenched, enclosed.

So he would often start thinking about one and then think about the other.

Or even just remember the light and then, not knowing he was thinking about either,

think of them both. Or perhaps it is the enclosure combined with the light that does this

as he also remembers remembering some

childhood infamy involving stolen whiskey and a briar bush.

He had set up a kind of fortress in a briar along with his friend.

He is truly amazed, can't believe, that he doesn't know where he's living now.

Over two years since he's seen him. And he remembers drinking stolen whiskey early one morning with this friend

his head gone before he knew it, then his stomach, but also looking up and seeing black branches backlit with white sky.

That had a returning quality too, that he couldn't seem to get away from and

there was some projection, constant in the back of his mind, of this consistent inescapable play of light.

Ms. Car

NOW, SHE IS SWIMMING. Back and forth and back and forth, until she stopped finally at the pool's edge, shoulders heaving. But it was only a minute or two's rest and then she kicked solidly off the wall, kicking underneath the surface, barely feeling the water stream past her body, finally breaking the surface and then, somewhat clumsily still, stroking through it. She tried to think of her arms as machines, going through a specific order of progress, but they would not always obey her request and were, finally, human, unable to deliver monotonous perfection on command. Still she fought it, and concentrated to bring each stroke down through the water correctly. There was breathing involved too, large quick breaths and slower exhalations bubbled into the water.

Around her, a scattering of other people swam in their lanes, a few points of interest for the lazing lifeguard. A muscular man chopped through the water fiendishly with a butterfly stroke that Car tended not to like, thinking it contained notion of mastery over the element. An elderly couple swam away from the others, in the "slow lanes," which, Car came to find, was more a communal designation than actual rule. The woman of the two was the better swimmer, in fact expert, and her skill showed a lifelong concern. She swam ahead, sometimes lapping the man, and would pause to watch over him. It became an understood fact that she was in the "slow lane" for his benefit. He rather appeared to be, like Car, learning how to swim. They were both awkward.

But though Car exhibited her youth in strength, they both applied determination to their task.

Car gathered these impressions in the few minutes she paused to rest, but soon expelled them and crashed back into the water, floating and flailing, sometimes efficient, sometimes not, slowly learning how to swim. She was learning quickly. It had only been a month since she joined the pool but she's come almost each day, enjoying the sport. Before she went the first time, she had vaguely envisioned a cool refreshment, a kind of daily wet cleansing. The actuality turned out to be steamy rooms and metal lockers. The temperatures were harsher, cold and shivering. Also a dehydration of her skin that she hadn't expected. Nonetheless she enjoyed it. It was indeed refreshing, actually, to push away in the water like that, to feel a grace of movement, to float.

She hadn't really swum since she was a girl, and she had begun hesitantly. There was a woman who worked there who gave her occasional pointers, told her in words what she looked like and what she might wish to correct. When she watched this other woman swim through the water, she tried to use it as a vocabulary to explain to her own body what to do. She was surprised to find the effort genuinely rewarding.

So that now, she was over her initial embarrassment and even tried to look a little professional in her exercise, mimicking the persona of the establishment—all business. Afterward she may have laughed to herself about the seriousness of the place, but it impressed her, actually, the mythology of personal achievement and discipline, the Olympic swimmers whose photographs were in the lobby, so that she is, now, pushing off the wall, conscious of her breaths, envisioning her arms and legs, swimming, to take her across the pool, back and forth and back and forth.

She swims for an hour, the rhythm of her strokes replacing, not counting, the time. The time is subsumed, finally, turned from a fourth dimension to a mental nth, one of work directed along an axis of action. There is distance, that of the pool's length, but is there? If she were to take all the lengths she has swum and lay them in a row, is that the distance? Swimming shifts her basic perceptions. She is somehow forced to contemplate as she never, upon stepping out of the pool's building and into a spring afternoon, quite understands the time that has passed. She thinks the word "relative" is a cop-out for the explanation; she feels an actual metamorphosis of some primary element but cannot state it, a limitation of language.

Yet still, each daily return to the building keeps this question. She enters the pool with it in her mind, only to find upon exiting that it had waited above the water, neither progressed nor moved, but somehow simply stood. On the bench. Next to her locker key. With her towel.

She swims with pleasure. The moment just previous to her entrance into the water is one of almost sexual anticipation. She thinks it may be a link to this other place, this "relative" place, one of body, perhaps, except the anticipation seems to be not for any act but a void, or perhaps the body remembers something the mind, not being able to state, does not. In any case the actual swimming is also conscious, effortful, a process of learning. It is a complex, in the end, and one that she enjoys participating in. The dive

into the water, the random slush and splish of first movement and then that sound's relaxation into a rhythm of arm and water, distance and turn,

turn and distance, forth

and back.

There were other ways she thought of it. A terminology of health and exercise, a mental clearance, a meditation involving repetition. She felt her limbs grow stronger. Also small aches which were gradually incorporated into her sense of herself so that they were finally no longer identified as such.

When a mass of children jumps into the pool she knows it is time to go. Kids' swim. Their hour named. She does not linger in the locker room but showers briefly under hot water. Sometimes the woman who gives her pointers is in the lobby, organizing children, or on a break—and they talk. She tells Car of how long she has worked there, her amateur swimming career, answers questions Car has, reminds her when membership dues should be paid, encourages her to look into some of the other classes. Car always says she'll look into them, but in fact is uninterested, as the woman knows. It's her/my job, both justify to themselves.

Sometimes Car goes up to the cafeteria and has a sandwich or a soda. She likes the view from the cafeteria, overlooking the pool. Initially when she discovered this, it made her self-conscious while swimming, but the seriousness of the place, its attempt to rid its image of frivolity relaxed her, so that she usually forgot the possibility of witnesses above. And even enjoys the view. She watches the children swim with plastic buoys or Styrofoam kickboards. Some took to it; others, and Car winced a little in recognition, weren't accustomed to their own bodies and moved their thin limbs spastically.

Car laughed. It was a show! vaudeville, clowns and dancers. Flustered instructors balancing kids who kick water into their faces. Graceful teenagers, lean with terrific bodies. Car ate it up. This and the movies had come to make up most of Car's major excursions out of her apartment. She enjoyed both but saw the joke. The rigor she and her husband had fabled themselves to live by, she had somehow created, in actuality, after they were no longer together. It was a possibility arising from solitude. As a couple she was not afforded, somehow not able to create a rut this deep, for eventually the other's pull shallowed one's involvement with self.

The weight had shifted now and she could, strangely, enter into these purely public spaces—the pool, the movie theater—because she was completely private, self-contained and the momentary or even illusory vibration that sounded between two people so fragile so impossible and there was time, so much time, spent chasing its possibility and to finally collapse inside, spent from the effort . . . It was a joke! a prank and one day thinking this way she is all but running to the pool, changing, jumping into the water with a violence that surprises the lifeguard who thinks to give her a warning but stops as Car's fury translates itself into the regular sight of her stroking, breathing through the water. She is coming along quite well, the lifeguard thinks, and her strokes are getting stronger and increasingly deliberate. The coordination of her arms and legs is becoming more and more instinctual. Though she differs in a certain intensity, the lifeguard notes, trying to articulate what, exactly.

Car herself thinks she appears different only as the novice is to the amateur. She feels she is learning and that there may be some unorthodoxy to her habit, but she is attentive to try to feel these out, make sure the mistakes do not pass unnoticed. She actively tries to correct and watches what the other swimmers, more advanced, do, and mimics them. The desperation she felt before getting into the pool is still there, acknowledged, but the impossibility of resolution is not lost on her. Her temporary answer, the response to its frustration, now, is activity and concentration. Arms and legs pushing the water until the wall, the turn, more stroking to the next wall, another turn. So forth and so on. So on and so.

Back and forth.

Distance and turn.

Turn and distance.

She is calmer when she finishes. Pacified? she wonders. The problems have turned intellectual again. The reaction using up the body, the residue made up only of mind. (Though, she worries, this is incrementally less and less so, so again she will have to change.) She wonders again where the time has gone, or more accurately, what has become of it. What it has become. She would return tomorrow, think it again.

She steps into the locker room, nodding to the elderly woman who is there again today. She takes off her swimsuit and twists it as dry as she can, places it in a plastic bag, showers, changes, dries her hair. She watches the woman go into the sauna who upon doing so says, "See you tomorrow." Car takes a generous look at herself in the mirror. A large industrial piece of glass, she likes looking at herself here. The mirror she has in her apartment is slightly warped, so here she thinks is the most accurate view of herself—so she even primps a little. She gathers her things and steps outside to smoke a cigarette, both guiltily and in rebellion against the health freaks inside.

Her walk afterward usually includes odds-and-ends grocery shopping. She gets home finally and makes a large lunch of noodles. Consciously tells herself to slow down, but wolfs it nevertheless. Window open with cool breeze, she rests and digests before tackling the work that will occupy her until late that evening.

Mr. Fog

THE HOUSE IS MOSTLY CLEAN. He is sitting in his armchair watching the water evaporate off the floor in front of him, where he has just mopped.

There are dreams he feels he must acknowledge, problems whose resolutions are impossible yet he cannot help dwelling on them. A hope says he just may yet. Is that what it is? he wonders. A hope for an end, or perhaps just a morbid fascination at the structure without foundation, still standing. Each limb cantilevering another and that in turn another, so that it stands on nothing but itself, an intricate flower which defying gravity he rips apart to find only an empty center.

There is the smell present, perhaps lingering from the mop, of ammonia and mildew.

Perhaps in his imaginings, in his mental talking and drawing of various shapes and constructions to describe his problem, he is creating not models and maps but other problems, and so, stepping back to see his progress, realizes all his efforts are simply increasing the empty space that the answers would, had there been any, occupy.

He had found the mop, gray, dust colored, in the garage. He had to clean the mop first before he could use it, and scrubbed it with bleach and soap.

Would a surgery of all that seemed unnecessary be appropriate? If he pulled apart these constructions and tried to only use what was crucibled as vital, the specific circumstances and situations stripped of all varnish and insight, would that somehow tell him Why? But what was necessary? It was another problem, also.

He had let the mophead just sit in bleach and water while he went around the house and swept. First, he swept, leaving little piles of pennies and dust throughout the house.

If he divided all his constructions apart from each other, cut and halved where the joints seemed weakest so they were put in separate containers, and then regimented his time and space to visit and explore one per set duration, was that the answer? Or was it only, again, an artificial engineering that would, if satisfying, do so falsely, from an incorrect belief in architecture to conquer space.

After he was done sweeping, he got out the dustpan and went through the house hunting for his piles. Sweeping them into the dustpan when he found them.

And even now, wasn't the abstraction of it the final complicity in failure. Shouldn't he name things? His wife, for example. His marriage, his friendship. The two losses. Or his house, this town, his armchair, the lake he sat beside. His job, the children, his colleagues, the desks, chairs, school.

Finally he went back to check on his mop. It was still gray. Perhaps cleaner but he couldn't tell. He prepared a bucket of soapy water.

But he had thought this way before, perhaps he had returned to it, perhaps he would leave and do so again, but there was a progress. My thinking is not a circle, he thought to himself, there is not a line but there is a progress through some substance. At some resting points between the murkiness there seemed vibrations or pockets of (accidental?) harmonies and he was either wasting or killing time in between or progressing . . . or, that the pocket was somehow also the murkiness in between?

Now, went through the house mopping. Occasionally coming across a dust pile that he had overlooked. Cursed, went back for the pan to sweep it away.

He is the greedy horse struggling between paradoxes, questioning if one is empty, the other wise. Perhaps he was, after all, thinking a circle, and only widening the radius until large enough it seemed a line, so distant finally in returns that he forgets, upon arrival, that each is not a new destination and only left: a faint nagging.

The last room, he uses the water generously. He purposely mops himself into the corner where his armchair is. Sits and smokes a cigarette, waiting for the floor to dry.

A useless way of thinking, he knows. Yet so much time is spent falling back into it. He will make his way in time, he has said so before, but there was a faith, ascended to in powerlessness, that he was on the verge of reaching for. Clutching? He remembers coming onto this question, realizing the oldness of it, the wisdom in keeping silent about it, but also, talking to him about it.

It was then that he caught the smell. A smell of light rotting, fungus. Maybe it was the mop. Ammonia and mildew, the smell reminded him of cafeterias and apartment building foyers.

The friend gently saying, Yes it is true, but I am here, you see. We, are here. And the joy in the saying, not frail and not a cold-centered joke. There. was. that. But what of it? In the religiousness of his thinking, in its very inception there was also a heresy that it was not enough, so that it was equally a descent.

The floor was dry. He took the bucket of water and set it out in the backyard. He made plans. Next weekend the garage. The weekend after that, the backyard.

So silence then was an option, as was whistling past the graveyard. But he knew bluffing was a weak feint. And silence, too, not as it seemed—that its surface held as much shape as a balloon, pressured by air.

He showers. Stepping out of the bathroom, seeing the light a little brighter off the floors, he allows himself a satisfied feeling.

There were other ways also, and he felt the need to leave the house, to change the problems from shapes and talking to muscles and ridges and water. He wanted to walk to the lake, or perhaps to the woods again where a small ravine carried a creek, drawing a shaky line through the woods. He wanted to be there now, immediately—perhaps if he was, it almost felt that then there would be a solution.

He walked through the house in his towel, dripping, going upstairs to his bedroom, also, peeking into other rooms. A luxury in the country, he could afford a house much too big for one person, so that there were rooms completely empty of furniture. Just, now clean floors and sunlight coming through undraped windows.

He grabs clothes quickly. He may still fall to it willingly, not helpless. Even now he knows a destination, a literalization of an abstraction of a pulp plot made literal wherein he will "solve" his "problem."

He puts on pants, slips socks and tennis shoes onto his feet, puts a T-shirt over his still wet hair, the water darkening it in streaks. He leaves the house in a quick walk through the cemented road now turning to gravel, then dirt, rising over a low hill. He begins to trot, jog, and then a full run to the lake.

He pauses to pant by the lake. He is holding the fat around his belly, wondering how long it has been in his adult life since he's actually run, even a jog, much less a full sprint. His head looks up from between his legs to the lake, which is still and brown, and his eye sees a perfect skipping stone.

Holds the stone in his fingers, rubs his thumb over its round, eroded surface. Fakes a throw, practicing. He wants to see it skip at least four times, maybe if he were to throw it just right it would make the other side of the lake. Its beauty unique here, where the rocks are either crunched dirt or shale that brittles and is too light to be thrown with any satisfaction. A good weight in his hands, a perfect skipping stone.

He envisions the skips on the still lake. Every skip causing noticeable ripples, several ripples from several points along a zagging line. He pulls back and launches with a good flick of the wrist. It kerploops directly into the water without a skip, a single, low-octaved splash.

Actually turns around to see if anyone saw him. The ripples from his one splash are spreading through the water and it seems to Fog like the group silence after something embarrassing has been said. He even laughs aloud a little. Abruptly picks up a cattail and strips it, letting its cotton dirtiness litter the side of the lake. He moves on, topping another hill, going down, losing sight of the lake.

The things were changing color and shape, the problems were rearranging to account for the air, now outside his house. Did he really carry them this way? like some various organisms in a petri dish, microscopic yet infinitely complex, reacting to light and action—stimuli—so that they reshaped and chameleoned to however he could look at them, containing multiple and overlapping properties which, like the fable of the equation, grew or shrunk by his observation in certainty and uncertainty.

Walking, he continues over some more dirt roads, cuts through someone's lawn, now, at the wood's edge. The short time at the lake was to gather his thoughts, he thinks, before he rushed into it. The speed was something he was contriving, allowing his deeper levels to prepare the trick for himself to witness, be surprised at.

Various trees covered the steep descent to the creek. He started down, soon fast and then faster. Gravity was helping him down, pushing him, actually, so that he was taking larger and larger uncontrolled steps, now beginning to fall, his legs staggering, barely in time to keep him upright. He remembered games at night played in a pine wood, hunt and prey games where you crouched behind tree shadows and then sprinted through the woods over a floor of needles silent and swift with your arms in front of face for always the fear of being clotheslined or battered by a low-hanging branch.

So that now he's doing the same, struggling to keep his legs below him and his feet crashing through the kindling twigs below but with his hands up pushing through the small branches that whipped at his upper body, unable to avoid them and hoping no force awaits, greater than his own gravity, to stop him with a sickening crack.

He is wondering how long could this possibly sustain, this gauntlet of branches and this vertical feet-to-ground but airy falling, when he sees the narrow clearing ahead where the creek is. His mind switches instantly to wondering how long it will last to wondering if he will be able to stop in time.

It is a shallow creek with a rocky, loose bottom and if he doesn't regain control he sees himself finally falling, really falling in his abrupt entrance into the creek. His feet will splash, making the water opaque enough to not see the relief of the rocks below and, unbalanced, he will fall hard and finally horizontal, into the water.

But the incline gentles at its bottom and though the ground of loose dirt and twigs slips beneath him, he tries to make his steps smaller and smaller, more control with each touch to the ground, so he finally stops, one sneaker dry on the bank and the other sunk in water. He wades through it to the other side.

The other side of the creek is an even steeper slope, a craggy rise directly up so that he realizes in a way he never had as a child, that the creek must have been once a true river, cutting away this valley, mellowing in time or perhaps wounded upriver by damming, as the town grew.

There is a way up the other side, he knows. An indentation of stone steps into the rise a half a mile to his right. But he wants to be at the top this way, so finds a nook with his now muddied tennis shoe. It is a true climb of about four stories. He puts a hand into another small jutting, knowing he is weary already and unsure if he can actually do it.

There are crevices and footholds that make the first five or six feet seem possible. This is maybe what makes him do it. The beginning of the climb is understandable, foreseeable, and he knows what his first several moves will be. He has them already envisioned when he reaches up and pulls himself off the ground, beginning.

The next steps happen easily enough, like a cat up a tree. He briefly notes that he hasn't seen anyone since he's left the house. That he lives alone. That it is a short but formidable uphill climb back out of the woods. That if he fell and was hurt in any way no one would look for him until he was missed, at work. Notes this briefly.

He is now past the point of his initial envisioning. His weight is on his left foot and he is scanning upward generally, left and right, for the next handhold. It feels much steeper than when he had begun. He is not yet scared because he knows if he must he could reverse the steps, retreat back down.

Then a small swing onto a short ledge and a few quick easier steps up. He is about nine feet up now and pauses as he can't see where to put his right foot. Now, he knows he cannot go back down and that some foothold or crevice back in the immediate past functioned as a valve, allowing him through but not allowing him back again. Fear stays held back for a few moments longer.

He is resting on one foot, the other not quite placeable anywhere. The slope enough so that he can lean his body into it with some comfort and stability. He measures that there is an equal distance up as there is down. He decides to continue and once again looks up, sees another handhold and reaches across his body to hold firmly onto this jutting. So that his weight now is balanced on two separate parts of the cliff: half on one foot and half on this other hand from which he is hanging.

Ms. Car

CAR WAS BUSY WITH WORK. Her assignments were picking up as she never refused anyone and was diligent to give what was wanted. Outside the work, which kept her in her apartment, she, though not very interested in display (and who would she show it to?), began a period of organization and cleaning. There were the minor repairs that she had had in mind since arriving: a torn piece of wallpaper, a loose piece of tile on the bathroom wall. She made a list and began her work. Over a series of days spaced evenly throughout several months, she wallpapered the kitchen, fixed a cabinet, regrouted and retiled the bathroom, painted several rooms, made bookshelves, fixed two leaks.

She alternatively saw these tasks as games and chores. Either way, they were actions she was compelled to complete and complete as well as she could. She was not entirely ignorant of the skills involved, nor was she experienced. She woke up on these "activity days" and would spend the first morning hour planning out her activity in detail. She began with what she knew of herself, her speed at various tasks, how much newness each endeavor entailed for her. Then she contemplated the task, thought about the tools she would need and the layout of her spaces, the area of her apartment involved: a specific room or cabinet. As she advanced through these activity days, she found that from each experience—though often one dissimilar to the other—if she paid attention, came a yield of some insight that could carry over into the next. So that when she was finally through, the fixed items stood throughout the apartment as a measure of her learning. The line began with the retiled bathroom and ended, triumphantly she thought, with the wallpaper in the kitchen.

After that it was a question of organization, routine, and maintenance. A few labels, folders, and a used filing cabinet created empty space on her desk and gave her a not-false feeling of professionalism. She took a little time to perfect the flow of assignment to draft to finished piece, so that her scattered and noted papers, for every moment of their duration in her apartment, were given places. A less detailed strategy was used for all other loose items—plates, cups, pots, toothpaste, books, tape, teapot, spatula, iron, playing cards, shoes. The idea was established—though Car was not really a tyrant, though she may have exhibited symptoms—of a pure and clean apartment. Car's efforts for maintaining this ideal were nonchalant. After she had actually taken the time to come up with places and strategies, she cared less about being vigilant.

Without planning to, she accompanied this organization of her apartment with a routine in her day. Though she kept her own hours, she woke early. She was slow in the morning. She entered the shower and shampooed her hair. While her hair was sudsed, she brushed her teeth. She would habitually spit her paste spittle onto her feet and dumbly watch the shower water sink it away. She soaped after this, and rinsed. Then she would lean her head into the wall and rest a long while. Finally leaving the bathroom she would, in towel, go to the kettle and boil water for instant coffee. While it was boiling she went into her bedroom, placed the towel on a chair, put her nightclothes under her pillow, and dressed, made her bed. Returning to her kitchen, she would prepare and drink her instant coffee and smoke a cigarette.

If it was an "activity day," she would proceed in planning. Otherwise she went to her desk to work. Her mind was still numb from sleep, so she would often sit inactively for half an hour. After another cup of coffee and perhaps a breakfast of toast, she would begin in earnest, clearly advancing through dull and slightly less dull translating and technical writing. This took her to the afternoon nearly always, though there were variants. She took a break at this point and read a book or listened to news on the radio. She spent some time on the telephone rounding up more work or updating whomever needed to know on her present work's progress. Then a few more hours of desk time until she left her apartment to go to the swimming pool and do some shopping, returning to eat a late lunch.

After lunch was less focused than before, and she often lost most of it lazing on the couch, reading a book, or napping. It was during this quieter time that she began to think again of traveling, or, after some time of this, it was here, in the late afternoon that she began to vary her days with weekly trips to the movies.

A democratic moviegoer, she usually chose as she had the first time, by whichever movie played at a convenient time. If she saw one she liked, however, she'd go see it half a dozen times, as long as it was still running. My husband had been like that—one day after she had seen a film for the fourth time: we both are happy to be in our ruts. They had talked about this often enough and they had even taken a pride in how stubbornly they had regulated their lives. It was a soft fact, not really completely true; they reinforced it, a mutual conspiracy against themselves—for they were as mad and chaotic as anyone she knew, would lose hours in various simple digressions—but she had enjoyed these conversations, regularly spaced, which shaped their thoughts about one another.

She had begun to think about him quietly, caging her thoughts with swimming, errands, and work. Yet there would be reminders, finally; light and place and objects—repetitions—that were inescapable.

How quickly she had come to know her apartment. With the routine, work, and repairs, the apartment became, of her life, a reference book and diary both. She knew that in the afternoon on a cloudless day, for a few minutes the sun would bounce off the opposing building's window and shine into hers. The voices of the neighbor's television would come quietly and regularly in the evening or, in contrast, the eruption of messier sounds from the family above. She heard them clatter through their weekend meals and in the hall on the way to some outing. Her reflection she came to know as specific to a few housings: in the bathroom mirror, curved so that she looked narrower; in the kitchen window at night; and in the spoon in her coffee which, licked after stirring, she played with mindlessly.

She did this somewhat on purpose, created this fact of familiarity, so that when she did leave her apartment, perhaps to see a movie or to go to the pool, the world would crash into her and she could feel knocked against. She prized this concussion, thought it was delicious and sudden, and it gave her, somehow, a sense of control. Gradually, she became more and more practiced in this dance of home and city, in and out. She came to conceive it as such: her own particular art. She saw herself experiment for its benefit, playact with colors and moods to see how to get the correct outcome, build up the cabin fever to taste fully the outside upon release.

For months she was preoccupied with this idea of controlled reactions, so that it took quite a while before she realized she had named it so as to distract. It was a game which, in essence, was played in isolation.

This did not come as a shock to her; she was familiar with her own loneliness, but the fact that she had hidden it this way revealed to her that the divorce had cost her more than she had previously acknowledged.

THE APARTMENT, IN EVENING, here where she was, darkening, came to a point when her desk light overtook the window light as principal illumination. After a moment, attuned closely to the surrounding changes, she thought, How funny it was, noticing, that it took so long, isolated as she was, to begin meditating on her situation. But perhaps very short, actually, as the dumb movement was in that other sense only, not unintelligent, simply silent in mind, and she maybe had needed its foundation.

She thought of her husband more openly now. He was a dreamer and practiced excuse-maker, somewhat like her father, she thought. Like her father, he had sometimes brilliant periods, flashes like a snake sprung that were followed by a lengthy time of retraction. She had married him for what she rarely had, or what rarely endured in her: his sense of his own conflict, which she thought upped the ante of her father. He saw a clash, which he himself admired, in himself, of a nihilism—which he could never decide was costume or belief—and a natural talent for affection and love. That she had lost interest in it was obvious to her, lost interest in him despite the comfort of it was, also, obvious. As she saw him play it out over their time together, she saw that he was lax in how he worked this conflict, that it had become easy habit, and this was what finally disgusted her. Or his final error, or hers, in that series that had made the conviction of divorce conclusive.

From this distance, she saw how they had met. She had been traveling, wandering, really, ending up in Argentina. He hadn't looked like a local but was putting up signs offering his services as a teacher of Spanish. She waited till he had left to examine his sign, judged him by its layout, and called him the next day. Then proceeded a six-month courtship that only once really took them out of the room where they studied. Mostly they came to know each other during their lessons: he would speak simply and she, exercising foreign grammar, would slowly make a stuttering sentence.

And then they had moved to Chicago and gotten married. Why not? they had both thought, and they grew more and more confident in their choice of each other, and then, at some point, the angle steeper down than up, less and less. Or that was rather too neat, and she remembered one night, coming home from the movies, wanting to say, just, only, Love is not possible, and say it abruptly, make the proposition clear, but was embarrassed that she had not progressed past such a statement. The thought had risen and faded in accord with its usefulness, throughout, even at that initial meeting as a kind of forewarning and then later as a concession, finally it became a dismissal.

Now she rises from her chair, puts on her nightclothes by lamplight, following out her routine, though differing slightly this evening. She goes into the kitchen, takes down a bottle of whiskey for a nightcap and, remembering, goes back to the other room for her cigarettes. She cracks some ice from the tray and pours herself a drink. The thought to travel keeps entering her mind. Before her husband, all throughout her life, including childhood, she had moved often. It was only in marriage that she had stayed, and comfortably stayed, in one place. At the time she had thought that the restlessness, the taunting Why not here if here or there? had ended, but in fact the marriage had.

Mr. Fog

IT HAPPENED TO BE a crude solution after all.

If it had been unthoughtful, why not? for the initial thought—the deciding upon rules—had been accompanied with a willingness. These were the rationalizations, but he knew, post the fact, he would have to face, maturely, that the game's machinery hadn't worked, wasn't fun like it was supposed.

What he had wanted to do, he now realized, was an act of religion, now revealed as superstition. Climb a rock. There, relief.

Now knowing this, his thoughts exposed to air, the magic trick was a graceless mirror, a reflection of the hollow bottom, the secret hoist. Useless. It hadn't been religion after all. Just more self-powered motions—him confabulated to be the Unknown.

He had tried to know himself. Useless. Cliff-hung, he realizes self-debating epistemology was a notch below teasing your seventh-grade love. He had taken all that time to de-evolve.

So what. Devolve, splay his limbs like a rutting animal, he would try again. Even now another game with different rules was offering itself. Oz had several neighboring countries. There were options out of every blacklist, he assured himself.

He only, now, had a few feet between himself and the top. He heard voices somewhere behind him in the valley. Spurred on by a desire to keep his solitude, he attacked the remaining few feet; scrambled, finally, pulled himself up.

At the top, he remembered the friend writing, after a visit, Why are you gone? Life is terribly short and very dangerous. Maybe we won't see each other again. And leaving, which may seem the slightest adventure, will end up your last, and with you gone, my last also.

The cliff had seemed a considered adventure. But perhaps hidden in it was the danger his friend had spoken of, because evidently at some time they had lost each other. He looked down the rock face and suddenly the fear that he had isolated and sidestepped came with an unshakeable force. He wanted to return home, but the only way back, though only a two-mile or so walk in total, seemed long.

He walked east toward the stone steps that made an easy walk down. He could go back down the ravine and then climb back up the other side. Or he could walk a bit further, a quarter of a mile more, and there was a bridge. He paused for a long time between these two choices, then, deciding he'd had enough of the ravine, walked toward the bridge.

He remembered how he would visit his friend. How they would begin with great happiness at seeing each other, open to a possibility, then as the visit—or even the day—passed, his friend would turn abusive and short-tempered.

Even with the strong desire to go home, he paused at the bridge. The sun was setting and the valley beneath was half shadowed and half a brilliant orange. They would sit in his kitchen, drinking. He would watch his friend's eyes squeeze tighter, and stepping no matter how softly, the eruption would come, Why did you come?

The bridge was black as the valley was fire. He crossed it, no longer seeing the colors, quickstepping, wanting to be home. After a few days, the friend would send him a letter, pleading a return or a forgiveness. Or it would seem. Upon closer reading it was insult disguised in apology, saying it was too bad, but he really did deserve everything he got.

His wife, finally, caring for him, spoke, To hell with him. He'll help himself or he won't. You can't do anything. She was right; it just didn't make any difference to him. He was lonely without this friend, who had been there the longest and was the closest. He was family. You didn't give up on family. He had said.

But what are you going to do? she had asked, correctly. Stand and wait, I suppose. You're being generous for nothing, she said, and left the room, angry. He was walking past the school now. A man was walking toward him, the school's band leader. The man considered Fog a friend.

But he didn't want to talk to him now, he simply wanted to get home, enjoy some of the long day's last light from his living room. The light would shrink on the floor, closer and closer up the southeastern face of his house, reddening then bluing then gone. But here the man was, coming up to say something.

And then the friend had given up in such a way that he knew there was nothing left to do. He was rejected so the small space that he had lived in, even that, taken, now, away.

Hello. Hello. Been hiking? Yes. Good weather for it. Yes, very. You don't live that far from the school, do you? No, it isn't far . . . How was band practice? Same as usual—say, you look a little pale. I think I may have overexerted myself. Everything alright. Yes . . . I'm going home now. Alright, hey Fog, remember . . . well, are you still up for helping me next weekend, work on my roof? . . . There's a fine dinner involved.

He remembered some offer of help he had given. Did he sound stuffy in front of this man? He really didn't want to help, but he also didn't wish to be alienated. Sure, of course. Next weekend, we'll talk this week about it. And they parted. He was sure he had left a bad impression.

He knew the man liked him; for some reason worried about him. The roof work was a good-natured ruse. Though he was proud, Fog liked it, endured it, because the man was genuinely good-natured. If Fog made clear he didn't want his help—both of them understood—that would be the end of it.

He was nearing his home now.

The interaction with the band leader had, he was surprised, put him in a better mood. All of a sudden, his thoughts about the man turned very tender.

He entered his house. He had forgotten he had cleaned it.

A breeze came through his windows, cooled by the sun's setting, but that had not carried out the lingering scents of bleach and soap. He took off his muddied shoes and set them on some newspaper. He sniffed his own sweat, which smelled of grass. The feeling as he entered he kept for a long time after.

HE CLEANS AND CHANGES his clothes. Again he leaves the house, this time heading into town. He vaguely thinks he may catch a movie or have dinner or a drink.

The band leader, like his wife, made him question his motives. Obviously they were right. Walk away. And he was just attracted to disaster because he had no pity. But, he denied it, it was something worth countering good advice for. Well, it hadn't been worth it, had it. It was one way to judge, and quite efficiently.

The main road doubled as an interstate. Here, he has a choice of four places. A diner, a Chinese restaurant, a fast-food restaurant, and a bar. Or, he could walk further into town where there is a movie theater and a handful more restaurants.

He goes toward town. At the movie theater he discovers that he's too late to catch the last show. He picks up a paper, so he will possibly return during the week.

Turning, he begins to walk back home. At the interstate, he decides to have a drink and enters the bar. He walks up to the bar counter. He doesn't see anyone at all, either behind the counter or seated. He waits, is about to leave, but someone comes, takes his order. He drinks two drinks in silence.

He leaves the bar and walks back home. Light-headed, he decides there is nothing better for him to do but to do his laundry. He takes his clothes and puts them in an empty plastic hamper, carries it downstairs. He puts a load into the washing machine, turns it on.

He goes into the kitchen and pours gin and tonic water into a glass. Takes it and a book and sits on the floor with his back leaning against the dryer. He does two loads before he goes to bed.

Ms. Car

THE APARTMENT, IN EVENING, here where she was, darkening, came to a point when her desk light overtook the window light as principal illumination. After a moment, attuned closely to the surrounding changes, she thought, How funny it was, noticing, to see myself in the choice of him and the choice of leaving. He had written, perfunctorily, told her of his situation in disguised terms. Uselessly she compared, sought to see if he was doing better or worse than she was, could only see that he was there and she here, living each with the ebb and flow of the other's ghost. He ended his letter, tone unchanged, by saying he missed and loved her and that he wished her well, a sign-off neutralized, now, from the emotion it may have once meant, did in fact once mean. She had gotten out of the directness of writing by a trick, a plagiarized sign from her father she knew he would recognize, and saw that the anonymous way he wrote was his way of responding in kind. Perhaps it had been cruel to write at all, but she thought he should know where she lived. In his letter were—as were, less detailed of course, also in hers—notes that things were, now, beginning to get along, must, would.

For herself, the routine was becoming less and less precise and she was staying up longer, re-finding the insomnia and nocturnal that she had left a long time ago. The work was also beginning, finally, to bore her. She knew she would have to eventually find options out of this, but it was something to do, something she had done when she didn't know what to do. And she would continue until it came to her, whatever *it* would be. She was anxious for it to happen but also tried to see that whatever came would also be a kind of waiting, as the time now was. So she relieved her impatience.

She went and saw, periodically, Sonya and Dan, who were, in their very different way, also waiting. Staring out into the now-dark night, hearing the family clatter to bed above, she vowed a superstition, to link herself to the gestation of their child. She would stay here until she saw it and then leave. It was as much of a calendar as anything else, more, possibly; the baby inside Sonya, its growth, as they attested to Car, was very real. There was even a date. So, Car told herself, the sense of time's arbitrary duration was not always this way; at least I started with some precise sense of it. But, finishing what she saw as a loose joke, I've always had a weak memory.

She would move again, in about a year, would probably travel again.

She was unsure if the pacts she was making this night were true, the final results delivered from months of body-sweating progress or simply the nocturnal dream she knew herself to often mistake for clarity. She went to the kitchen, eyes open but not necessarily, and found the whiskey and a glass.

Sometimes she did envy others' memory—her husband's, for instance, (unfortunate, she usually thought) talent for nostalgia—as she knew there were times, as now, when not remembering contributed to her homelessness. She remembered not remembering, possibly, which, like seeing an empty plate, taunted her appetite. She remembered once, when her husband had, by a gesture, made it apparent to her that he was seeing again some other distant moment, and that it comforted him. Disguising herself, she had asked his thoughts and he confirmed the suspicion, though he could not say what he remembered. He reasoned it was a product of addition, of events fit together in lucky harmony with one or more other events, other evenings. Car envied the sediment in his brain, the strength he got from a connection but made light of it, told herself that forgetting also had its comforts.

In that acquiescent feeling she stretched herself out in her chair. She was completely awake. She realized she was chain-smoking, gagged lighting another cigarette but wanted it, kept smoking it. A memory not as far back unshielded now in her. In all this time, as the room darkened, there was a figure being brought out, remembered. She did not struggle with it, knowing an effort to find it would, as if aware, cause the memory to scuttle back down its animal hole.

Her husband, it seemed to her, had recounted all his memories to her. She even knew his first memory, or so he had thought it: He was the son of a soldier stationed in Korea and, from all accounts later gathered, a whore (that had been his word) turned wife, his mother. This first memory was some picnic the family had gone to, in some spring, on some mild mountain, overlooking some city, in some night. There was no one, now, to confirm the memory or detail its vagaries, but he demanded of her to believe in it so she, not caring, did.

Fog said, We had eaten canned beans cooked with tomato juice. Afterward, the fire where we had cooked our dinner was dying, and my father took out a pocket knife and poked holes into the aluminum can the beans had come in.

The father then, in one quick scoop, gathered up glowing coals into the can. Fog said he only later realized that the trick was one performed before (otherwise he had thought it a miracle unique to his father and unique to that one night) when his father brought out a long piece of thick twine. His father said, Now watch this, and began whirling the can in a circle, all three of them growing excited and more excited until his father began, Fog's word: whooping, dancing in and out of the circle he had made out of embers.

She had heard this story so often, she knew when he was going to tell it from the simple pattern of a company's or evening's conversation. She knew, finally, all the memories he could articulate and they were legion; it seemed to her a life's worth, or perhaps two lives', as she could only answer specific questions and could not draw a story of her past, or, rather, didn't want to. So perhaps Fog made up the balance.

She now remembered the figure she had seen. Or remembered where and what he was wearing. He was wearing a business suit in Midtown, and those two details usually sufficed for Car. But he was familiar. It had been last week; now, she almost places the encounter.

The most she was willing to do was bring her husband as near to the memories as reality would allow; she brought him to her parents' house. She could not see how he constantly measured time in memory. He saw the present, when happening, written in the past tense. Or perhaps what she couldn't understand was why he kept time this way. His method seemed to take as a given that such a thing existed, purely was/is/will be—and wasn't an incidental of calendar page.

Whoever the figure was that was eluding her memory, it was someone changed, almost disguised, from who they once were.

For herself, there were only shifts, patterns, which occasionally could be identified as what? moods, complexes, simply patterns, perhaps, which accounted for her, now, in her apartment, after her divorce, in a period of waiting. Her apartment was one measure; the swimming pool also, its own flux; work still another. But that was very clean, and sometimes she did think this way, which perhaps as a singularity was, also, what her husband did. But there were also concurrent existences which did sum up, did testify to a pattern, but were not said, only, as *one.*

She felt a break, a period now entered of summing and casting away. She would fulfill her promises to herself. Where would she travel, she was not sure, nor did she know, other than doing what was necessary, how she would spend her days.

She knew she had lived a series of destinations and this particular, now, her apartment, would not be the last. There were questions of practicality and whim that would have to be answered. Where and How. But as for Why, it did not need an answer, or, she felt, it was redundant with the act of going.

She did not feel her husband simple, definitely their marriage had not been. But the end of their time together, well, she felt that to be necessary. The final move, the divorce, was crystal; she had regrets but no doubt that she had wanted, thus needed, to leave, and that fact buffered her against the doubt—slightly but it would have to do.

Her eyes, tired, blinked. Lights had come on across the shaft. The television was turned on in the next room and she could hear the morning news.

She had stayed up all night. She rose and stretched, walked into the next room, idling, not just yet ready to sleep. She went to her desk and listened to the day gear up around her. The apartment, in morning, here, lightening, came to a point when the window light overtook the desk light as principal illumination. After a moment, attuned closely to the surrounding changes, she thought, How funny it is, noticing, to see the many instruments of measuring time: spring her apartment her body pool laps Sonya's child the light.

PART TWO MARRIAGE

To crib the imagery of an acquaintance, to paraphrase lengthily and restate the above, it would be like an island managing to throw out from itself with whatever enormous effort and depletion of certain hoarded materials enough matter to touch, however tenuously, a main body and thus become a peninsula. If one could find the causeway only at lowest tide—the walk to Mont. St. Michel—could this still with benevolence be called Grace? I suspect redundancy: benevolence surely is Grace, or its central atom.

—Coleman Dowell
from *Island People*

Jim Fog had convinced himself that he had painted on top of nothing. So that he didn't understand when Judy Barton came to him as he was leaving, saying, The house looks great, and he, not understanding, not remembering, because the house wasn't connected to his labor.

To relieve him, she said, The paint job. It looks fine.

He was woozy from the drink, stepped through the door, and she followed. Thank you, he finally said. Snapping also, at the end, How do you know Frank?

She was at the far end of the porch by then, and answered, Let's go for a walk.

I was going home.

Oh. Alright.

No, I didn't mean, it was just, it hadn't occurred to me to do it differently. I, I didn't . . . yes. Yes, I would.

Good.

She led him out to the lake, she leading him to the places one season former he had known so well, using his environs to map himself, failing utterly. They rounded it; he found the lake shrunken from spring, and it surprised him. He laughed.

Answering her look, he said, I've been so wrapped up in myself, it's silly, but the fact that, this lake I walked around every day, several times a day. And it's, now it's, and now it's smaller. It's shrunken. By August I guess it'll be gone.

Yes, she said, and he didn't feel ridiculed. His statement was allowed and he knew they were flirting.

She led him further, the path closing into the wood. Do you know where this goes? Yes, I've taken it many times. You should lead then. No, I enjoy following. They were both warm with drink. She took his hand and they continued silently. Then she stopped and sat on the ground. He sat also and looked up. A negative of some childhood memory was in front of him, confirming that he was not there, not anymore there; instead it was night.

She took his hand and led him to a tree, which she turned from to face him. She told him to make love to her, which he did obscenely.

He woke to Loneliness, Jealousy, and Need. These three, fat Frank Exit gave name to, as if, by naming, specific and full account was given of his constant yearnings. Principally those three. If he were aware of his dreams, he'd say they accompanied him there also, if only as that which he escaped from. But when he was conscious, their fact was always. He was aware of these emotions and for knowing his misery, was slightly less miserable. Because Frank's defeat was surprisingly thus partial, his smugness offered a thin (and waning) barrier against all-out depression and he lived—scurrying for an answer before this final vestige was gone and he was left in a forever dark and heartless chamber.

Summer, for instance, was relentless. He would frequently go to spectacles—that was the only word for them—to bathe himself in a wash of forever-concluded desire. A movie, a baseball game, or, best, a fight. The aching temporarily relieved by a sweaty muscle sweeping air on the way to contact. Lotus breath sugaring his tongue, there was again, always, the crowd. He'd sit far from the given action so that the allowance was thus greatest, and scope. Too early, never bored, pathetically and visibly eager.

He made sure, by some miraculously present instinct for survival, that his looking—his prowl—was only done away from the office. That was the extent of his shame, or, the extent to which it held sway against his other desires. A concert in the park. There, a man or woman, forehead oily, eyes attractively bright, all—for Frank—potential! Loitering outside the theater, leaning his bulk against the building, a cigarette toked upon as if to hide himself behind smoke, eyes watching. The exact possibility unclear but he was *sure* it was in the next moment, accident, contact . . . but—nothing.

Still he looked. The car's window rolled down, a hot breeze came across the shopping center's parking lot. For twenty minutes he sat in the heat, pooling sweat, watching the crowd come in at the end of a workday; the kids already there doing as much as he was—with much more reason. Men and women nauseatingly fresh. Clothes without wrinkles walked toward their advertised progeny. To be so confident, he thought, to be so unquestionably *of,* but—the complications! She didn't love him, they were bored with their children, he wouldn't take his medication, he was really bankrupt, she couldn't understand why he wanted to, he didn't love him. But to Frank, this was all relative to the fact that she spoke so casually to the man in line next to her.

He levered himself out of his car, backside drenched, and slowly made his way to the food court. He ordered a fried wonton and a Coke, threw a penny into the indoor fountain, sat on its edge. Since there was a woman across the marble plaza, and—since, though her face was out of focus he could still guess her sleeveless blouse's material—he fell in love. And when she left, the young mother with stroller, beautifully proven sexual, was the next. For variation, the loud voice and overheard (not stupid) joke was his friend to death. In plain moment, the landscape became a glossy magazine and he dutifully and ecstatically fucked.

And yet and so, when the viewing wasn't enough, the dead void took him to deeper needs. He wanted just contact, to be next to the running city, enveloped, standing at a point, in the field's rush. He drank at a bar in the airport. There, among the melodrama of hellos good-byes and anxious lateness, he sat—not waiting—among all who most assuredly were just. He wore a moderately expensive suit and had several stories ready for the barkeep, who never asked. He told himself he went just to look, and acted, he thought to himself, to not be seen. He pantomimed a delayed businessman with casual but frequent looks at the clock. Silent sighs while tamping his cigarette. He fretted over the details of this theater of the invisible, but lied to his consciousness and—sabotaged every performance. For so open was his need, so blind was he to himself in these safaris, that all who were watched by him, all who noticed him, were compelled, without exception, to deny him. And Frank, thinking he was unseen when in fact his eyeball and brain were only too evident, tragically misread his environment.

Eventually, after several hours, he got up, paid his bill, took a walk past the baggage claim, found his car, looked expectantly at the woman who took his parking stub, and drove home. For a while, before bed, he sobbed into his hands. He then fell asleep—quieted and dreaming.

WHAT SARAH CAR COULD SAY, she did, however little that was. She wanted to make an effort, at least that, at last that. Out the window she could see the heat solid in the air and later would be out directly in it. Summer threatened her with ending, by beginning, and she felt her inefficiency up to then was an increasing liability. But thinking so, she found, did not change things.

The square of her window, cut again into four, showed straight into an inscrutable whiteness. So she stood up, looked instead onto the street which, peopled, allowed her to flatter her powers of understanding. She was about to go out into it, but didn't. She kept looking around for something, felt sweat accumulating, and went to open the window. Traveling! That would ease this mindlock. Or keep changing the view from the window so that it would seem . . . that was it always, she understood. And the feeling of the trap which she had been born into and which age had only allowed her to perceive . . . was but one context which she used.

She got a glass from the cupboard and filled it with ice and water. It stood on the table in front of her, a cylindrical mimic of the window, sweating. She placed it against her closed eye, first one then the other. She cleaned the glass of its condensation and peered through it to her distended world. As she put it down, she listened to her environment become static, and she involuntarily lifted her shoulder to wipe sweat from the side of her neck.

Searching for some release she moved the glass of ice water to the edge of the table. For a moment the potential for crashing it to the floor held her rapt.

She had not opened the window, though she remembered she had moved toward it to do so. She approached it again and in so doing, knocked the glass over onto the table. She watched the water slipping to the sides of the table, curve down its edge, then drip to the floor. Seeing the ice cube gently skid a short path, she thinks of bobbing for apples.

She puts her hands behind her back and, without thought, judges her height to position herself. She leans over the table, mouth agape, and aims for the ice cube which, frictionless, pops from her lips and skitters away. She nudges it with her nose to a more central position, its volume diminishing; on her nose skin a single bead as legacy. She goes for it again, small enough now to be subjected to the vacuum of her mouth; then, in the trap of her teeth the sound of a single crunch—a testament to victory but so small! But one crunch sound!

From the freezer a complete—new—cube is brought to the table. As Sarah positions herself, she realizes she has never questioned the dimensional lie in "cube." And by what right would she? she thinks on her way down, and when her mouth touches the ice, the proposition is forgotten forever. The previous attempt had taught her caution and hypotheses of position, which testing, she proves successful but not without a satisfying difficulty. The ice cube is in her mouth. Not one, nor even two, but three! solid crunches of the primary variety followed by the numberless fade-out of secondaries.

She sat down, the cold painful to her gums. The window still was closed and the coolness in her throat was soon gone. Around her, the heat oppressed. Something stopped her from going to the window yet a third time. All that was done was a looking up, again through the window, to the sun—which now in position of her sight—sanded the sky to a hard color. The room was filled with it, and as her eyes scanned the details shown, all seemed, by their retreating shadows, prostrate to the heat.

The refrigerator within distance, she stretched her leg out and nudged open the door. The cold sank to her naked foot and the food gave off a numbed smell that neither countered nor increased her appetite. She closed the door, retracted her leg, and then for several moments did not move at all. She felt, if she *willed* it, the company of her surroundings—by not seeing, feeling, or hearing them, it—would leave her and she would find an utterly complete solitude.

She brought a hand from her lap and patted the water left on the table.

The night previous she had gone to a bar. She had gotten drunk without conversation, gotten home without incident, and yet still woke embarrassed. She sat for a long time more, and the only thought that dully repeated was to pour herself yet another glass of ice water.

Jim Fog

THERE WAS A POINT, in the beginning of that summer, when I got lonely. It was a sudden emotion and I hadn't expected this version of it, which started to choke me. And I didn't count on summer, which, because school was out, left me with time to myself. And, I didn't have the stomach to continue what I was doing. This, which made all the difference, I recognized later. At the time I had a different view. What I had thought was that I had come to a place, a quiet place, perhaps one of a long review, maybe a final rest. But I had planned on staying in this place for a while. The "place" as I keep calling it was just the slowtime after my divorce, and the meditations made when one suddenly finds oneself isolated. I thought I saw this clearly and accurately and perhaps with some self-pity, but I allowed myself that, since, if I was keeping it to myself, I considered I had the right to do so.

My general plan was to review the path that had led up to this place. Review the memories, and since I had many memories, I thought this time would last quite a while. But in fact it was very short, and if there are dates to such movements, and if it began with my divorce and ended at the time I met Judy, the whole thing lasted less than a year. Less really, a few seasons. And it started with the summer, which turned out to be, for me, decisive.

At that point, when I got lonely, to say it. When my stomach gave out. I didn't know exactly why, then, though it didn't take much figuring to see why, later. But at that point I decided to do two things. I decided to give up looking for a friend whom I'd lost a long time ago and whom I was hanging too many hopes on. And I decided also to accept the friendship that was being offered to me at that time. I mean I decided to see the people who were in that town who had said they were interested.

So I went over to Bill's house. I had agreed to meet and work on his roof. At the time I had accepted this invitation, it was more for the proper look of it; I told myself I would go through the motions of civility. But later, when I actually went over, things had changed, and I was willing to become involved with whatever they had to offer.

I went to work on the roof, but somehow—Bill's sleight of hand—we had ended up in his backyard, talking, relaxing. Nancy, the producer of the local radio news, his wife, in one lawn chair. Bill, leader of the high school marching band and player of Dixieland and big band, sat in another. The grasshopper sounds and there was beef grilling. It was an awkward afternoon and memorable, to me, because I was still conflicted about my involvement.

Bill was a generous person. He wanted to be kind to me. Nancy was his wife.

I mean to say that she likewise was generous, but she was a goodish Samaritan and it felt to me like hypocrisy. I am probably wrong. And even now I can see errors or possible other ways. Bill was less sharp, and the oozing field of comfort that surrounded him was one of a man relaxed and settled with his failures and sins. So, another admission: this was possibly why he comforted me.

She was generous because she lived with Bill and had lived in his mannerism, which condemned her to act kind.

But she was probably more witting of this and railed, in her own way, against it. How it ended up with me was that she would come to face me and ask flat-out, "Are you lonely?" I answered that I was, but that I was also, more or less, coming out of a slump and was making do. But my fumbling answer, had it been clear or even accurate, was unnecessary. It was a rhetorical question, and if she meant it as an offering of therapy or friendship, I always took it as an accusation of selfishness.

But in the shade of that first afternoon little of this was seen. I was sullen, ungrateful to Bill's overtures. We had some drinks. Every once in a while Nancy would get up to tend to the meat or Bill would go into the kitchen and bring out some more ice, pour some more whiskey. My glass had Snoopy on it. Nancy and Bill were sipping from coffee mugs. It does seem very domestic, doesn't it? It was at least familiar enough, to me, that I soon felt the distance that I had either pretense to, or actual feelings for; well, I soon felt that if it was the former then it was uncharitable, and if the latter it would suffer no damage if I kept it more to myself. So we talked.

I mentioned that I had grown up in that town, many years ago, and I said that I had some classic feelings about home and this was the reason for my return. Bill and Nancy had both grown up in small towns. He in Pennsylvania and she a little further north, there in Ohio. They had met when they both were in college at Ohio State. I mentioned that I had lived in Chicago and before that in Argentina and they murmured sensible things about my worldliness, taking it all with a grain of salt, as it goes, and joked because I had gone away and come back and it confirmed for them that they had done right and wasted less time by staying put. We started there and went on, getting to know each other, then, after a time, pitching those assumptions gathered into other topics. We talked.

That attempt stuck with me. I think it was the last preliminary to the involvement. Well, the involvement had already begun, so it wasn't that. An echo or the final denial, or defiance against something long ago already begun. One more example of the distance that I still doggedly wanted. I wanted there to be that distance. As if to say: I was here in a lab coat and they were in the maze. To set up an inside and outside, with me straddling. But there wasn't an outside; we were all together in one place.

ANOTHER DAY, SOON AFTER, there was a day with good weather. And on that day, we really did work on Bill's roof. Or at least I did. It was a simple job of cleaning his gutter. It was easier for me to do it than Bill, who was healthy but not agile. Both Nancy and Bill were in their sixties. At first I was a little confused at how it was going to work, because the picture of Bill on a ladder was immediately tragic. But I then saw that I was supposed to do the work on high and that Bill was going to hand me what I needed and stay on ground level. This was embarrassing for both of us, and slightly outside of Bill's character, I thought, for it reduced our relationship immediately to that of worker and supervisor. But Bill was probably a little blind to this and did really think that we were equally sharing the work. Or convinced himself that this was true. The first half hour I took the trash from his draining and put it in little plastic bags that I handed down to him. It was apparent enough that Bill didn't need to be there and after another half an hour I told him so. He asked if I was sure, because he actually had planned on painting the house too, and if I was sure, he'd begin on that. I told him it was a waste of his time and that he should go ahead, which he then did.

This made more sense to me, then, that we were actually going to share some work on the house. I had just, by accident or misnaming, been led to believe that we were going to share one task, when in fact it was two separate tasks. I understood if he had done it purposely why Bill would have done so. It was a simple slip to say he wanted some help, and to hint that the work would be more like a community affair than the lone job of a hired hand. I could have felt used, but Bill I think knew that it was a chore in either sense, and that perhaps I would even prefer this way. And it was true that I did.

Anyway, I liked the work, which was simple and also lifted the burden I had felt from the start of our relationship. In the short time we had spent together, a pattern had been set: I was always coming over to their house and eating their food and drinking their liquor. Bill probably had thought of this too, and he was offering me a way of balancing debts. It was certainly easier than inviting them over to my house, which was, at that time, a scary prospect. So it was a slightly deceiving matter of utility, this action of Bill's, but I was happy that he had done it. It cleared the books in a very practical way. Whatever its initial slight perjury or even its condescension, it was a logic of Bill's that I could recognize and therefore accepted. It made me closer to him to know him in this way.

Nancy came out and gave me a glass of ice water. We didn't say much. She just called up that she had a drink and I came down and drank it. In that way, she too confirmed the situation—that I was working off some kind of debt. I was treated like she would have treated any repairman, kindly but with an eye to the job. This made it all clear, it made it apparent that everyone knew how it was going to be so I therefore set to the task with a lot of energy. If this was my repayment, then I thought I might as well perform my bargain's end honorably. But in fact it was a very simple job and I was done in another hour.

Having come to see it as I think they saw it, having come to see how it was set up, I had a strange but common enough thought: that I was getting off too easily. And, secondly, that this was also their construct. It is always better to have someone in your debt than its opposite. Among friends, it would be best if it were always equal, but that didn't seem possible just yet.

I deposited my tools and the ladder in the garage and walked around the house to where Bill was painting. Well, maybe you see now how it was going to go. Bill wasn't painting. He had covered, somewhat badly, a section of the wall, but I found him sitting on a lawn chair, sipping a drink. It was making more sense. I've mentioned our difference in age—they were in their sixties and I was thirty-six at the time—which was something we never talked about but was obviously underneath everything. At that point I don't think Nancy or Bill, at least not Bill, had any of this planned. Not obviously, for it was too open and would have been too rude for them. It was an accident that the appearance of their need became so open. It may seem I'm contradicting myself by saying that simultaneously they had thought about my labor as repayment and also that they were not aware of obliging me. But I think the idea of my painting the house was not in their plans at all, and I was the one who stepped in, saw how we would all benefit, and volunteered myself. You could say I was duped, but the final tally may say otherwise. And anyway, all this—from the initial invite to my ending up painting their house—was made of clicking instants of thought and not as clinical as this may make it seem. It was the sudden shifting of weights that is unnoticeable but is how the machine works. They protested of course, but perfectly so, and I spent the next hot days, very enjoyably, painting their house.

I would come around six in the morning, to start in and avoid the heat. They had a large house. I was determined to do a good job painting it. Concerning my own life, I couldn't be lazier. But working for someone else is different, and also, as I have said, I had other reasons for making sure it was done right. It was a chore, and one that I wasn't at first used to. The first morning, I felt the strain rise in my back and creep into my arms. I took an hour break at the hottest part of the day and stopped around four. Afterward, I ate the dinner that they gave me and we drank and talked until late. I thought the alcohol might stun my back, toxify my muscles, but I soon realized I needed those nights to be as they were as much as the days.

In the course of that time, while I was painting their house, much changed in our relationship. It was easy to use the playact that I was working for them when it was just a quick two-hour labor. But as I was painting their house—and I purposely lengthened it as long as I could—we were obliged in different ways. They had to be grateful and I had to show that the charity was nothing. Simply, we had to become friends to make the whole thing agreeable. So that subtle shift, too, was made. The food Nancy and Bill served was a little better than previously, and they were fast at making conversation. I too was quick to show I wasn't tired and, in fact, the actual painting worked a therapy I hadn't expected. I found myself surprisingly cheered up. The whole thing turned out to be, quickly turned out to be, very involving and pleasurable.

On the last night—it was midweek—I invited them to come over for drinks that weekend at my house. They answered yes immediately and skipped quickly over to the next topic. It is nothing, inviting friends over, but it did make me nervous. Though the movement's direction had been unalterably set by then, I was still, to myself, mimicking defiance.

THAT WEEKEND WHEN THEY FINALLY came over, I struggled. It seemed obvious that the large house was carelessly lived in, a sign that the lodgings were taken for granted, a sign I took of myself. I was makeshift. The furniture spoke of this, not laid out for guests. I recognized this only after they left, chided myself at the easy correction, now missed opportunity. One armchair facing only space was not a dinner table.

What did it mean for me to live alone? It had meant, in the previous season, a life directed interiorly, shaved of all other perspective. The house was set up as a simple machine, a portal made of comfort and minimum decoration, to transport me to the nation where I had lived, named Mind, peopled by characters called Memory and Dream.

Am I so simple, I asked myself, that I've run out of fuel, that is: ego, so that my machine has broken, leaving me marooned. I had wished to rebel against this idea, to believe in the purity of a hermit vision. But in the end, I got lonely. That understanding gutted me.

I was not who I had thought I was. The revelation was no less painful because it was common; it was specifically painful because it was common. Seeing myself incapable of succeeding in my ambitions, I was forced to turn practical. I saw it as a step down. I had so admired my friend and my wife, who did otherwise. But there, it seemed, it was. That weekend, looking at my options with a cold eye, I finally accepted my new course, determined now not to lose everything.

But since I was turning practical, I tried to remember that self-knowledge was a myth of varying degrees of falsehoods. When I met Judy at Bill and Nancy's house, the new course of decision was fresh in my mind, but I was wary of turning her into a symbol.

I MET JUDY ON A SATURDAY night, about two weeks later. Bill and Nancy were having a party, in part, they said lightly, to show off and celebrate the house painting. If I regard the whole thing as a sequence of steps which I am pulling out of history to show you, then the final step, which locked it into place, was the night of that party. I am making my observations from somewhat a far distance, I understand, and it's easier, from here, to say this and this is what happened. But if you think about how one actually becomes friends with someone, how you meet your wife, or how you come to be in the chair where you're sitting, *and* you want some answer, and you are desperate to make some sense of it, you will find a story. And soon enough you, if you're like me, will be—for you have no choice—satisfied with it. Well, you may think I'm no expert on satisfaction, but I can say that I really do, now, think this is how it happened.

But having said that, to be honest, I don't think I'll ever get used to the concurrences of that night. Afterward, after leaving the party, I remember buzzing with the thought I might escape after all. That some remnant of the old possibility was still open for me. It didn't take long to find out this wasn't true, but nevertheless, still a disappointment. And for a short time, it was even worse, and felt like a slap in the face, because, you see, it had for a moment seemed possible that something new was about to open up for me.

To speak of the coincidence of that night—which was the simple coincidence of meeting someone who knew Frank, my friend—would say nothing. After all, how many people have met their wives or husbands through friends, or friends of friends. Matchmakers who are drafted into the occupation simply by time and position, by chance meetings. But I had not been to a party in over a year. Had specifically come to this party as the last step in a series of deliberate decisions to exorcise my loneliness. And furthermore the friend whom I had felt closest to all my life, and who had sunk into a bitterness that left no room for me—that he would be the matchmaker! It was the closest that I've ever felt to religion, and if that night had only delivered what appeared of its potential, I don't doubt that I would be a believer. The fact is, however, for all that, nothing changed. I went straight onward and this abracadabra night I remember as nothing more than an astonishing aberration.

Sarah Car and Frank Exit

AT FIRST, SHE'S A LITTLE PUT OFF by the bright light of early summer. Like the still-alive teenage part of her that can't stand to be happy kicks in and says This sucks. But four steps more from the subway exit and she's into the sun; the adolescent bravery dying, she barely notes, like it always does.

Still, she's kept her fair share of edginess, she thinks. She's thirty-four and the year before had divorced her husband of seven years. Not a sweethearts' marriage, but as close to a shotgun's as can be without the pregnancy. Now in New York City, working a job—more or less self-employed, thank god—that no one could say isn't a complete dead-ender. She's a freelance fact-checker, copyeditor, technical writer. Which means she's a hack-of-all-trades and paid like a dishwasher. Well, she had aimed for the land of Edginess and ended up in the limbo of Ambitionless. Enough of what passed for middle-class street cred to get her through anonymous bar talk, but not much else.

Today, she has to run an errand in Manhattan and has limped out of bed, not quite hungover and not quite healthy. It's that and the leftover and insidious back anthem of Edginess that makes her initially growl at the sunlight, but the sheets of warm yellow bouncing off the skyscrapers' curtain walls throw their fairy dust on her, and the beast is charmed quiet.

She gets a coffee and decides to rest on a bench. Doesn't have to be anywhere, just eventually. A thousand thirty-minute lunches are at that moment being conducted all around her. She's touched by the secretaries and suits walking out of revolving doors. Instant smile as the sunlight hits them. Easygoing people with husbands and wives in Westchester, Ditmas Park, Flushing, and Hoboken. With an effort, she stops herself from going insane with envy.

The sunshine and the smell of good fried food and heavy sauces which make up everybody's takeout are all around her. She forgets about herself, thankfully, in the pace of all its details. Dotting the field of beef curry over rice and tasteless California rolls and jumbo hotdogs and mayonnaise-drowned turkey heroes are the Tupperware and homecooked lunches of those who keep clean homes. In an undisciplined way, she tries to observe one at a time. Take one suit and one mustard-filled knish and watch the entire sitcom of chewing from beginning to end. But the plot bores her even though switching to some other luncher has just more of the same.

She re-fields it one last time, and makes it into an art-house flick. Not too arty, just enough to not make you feel cheap at the end and maybe a little sad. The ten-minute character sketch enlarges to a three-hour slow-mover. Subplots and chance meetings are built up and resolved tastefully, with enough randomness to pacify her quota for complications. At the right moment, a few hours later, she notices the sun has shifted slightly and infinitely sadly westward.

She looks around and rolls title credits over the emptying scene.

Getting up and stretching, a sweet melancholy from her game lingers. A received idea from some southern novelist sighs into her ear—Days are getting longer—and boosts up her spirit a little more.

She walks toward the building where she's to drop off some paperwork, the almost-forgotten excuse for this day in the sun. There's something inescapable about the light, growing orange at the speed of a clock's minute hand. She realizes the game has this side effect: she can't escape her movie. The titles have rolled by even while the second feature has been mercilessly projected onto her eyeballs. She shudders and is about to whistle in appreciation at this diabolic self-torture, when a figure in the distance jams the take-up reel and forces the whole apparatus to shut down permanently.

This guy's someone she knows but can't quite place. He's different, too, from how she knew him, almost disguised. He is covering his share of sidewalk with an admirable pragmatism, walking toward her, backlit by that now-forgotten afternoon light. At twelve paces away, she's about to stop him, vocalize her surprise, when he turns and walks into a building. She catches up and looks through the glass doors, watches his back get smaller and smaller, until it eventually disappears into an elevator. She feels vaguely insulted.

New game. Memory.

This one she also doesn't want to play but, once begun, there's an inevitability that her mind, like a ball thrown upward, gravitates toward.

Not to say she doesn't fight it, throw the ball back up every time it comes tumbling down . . . Back in her apartment that evening, she flicks on her desk light. There's a comfort to the pile of papers, as dull as the work may be. It is, at this moment, her main proof of participation. She spends a few hours adding to the pile of papers on her right, diminishing the pile on her left, trying not to think about the man in the suit. If she would stop her work at just that second, and try to scrape her brain's bowl and dig up the answer, she knows there's equal chance of it sifting out as there is it being lost forever.

She doesn't take the chance and lets it lie fallow, confident it's there and that slow processes will bring it to the foreground most surely.

And that's what happens. A few weeks later, at the opulent bookstore, she's indulging another habit: leafing through travel books.

And at that moment, whatever neural fluid, composed of X-part nostalgia and Y-part memory, sloshes around the correct synapse and the answer fires home.

Yet she can't be absolutely sure. She needs to confirm with something more concrete, so she drops her book, leaves the store, and catches the subway uptown.

Inside the building the man had disappeared into, Sarah registers a familiar combination of lushness and dust. The vestibule is empty save for three somehow flourishing ferns spaced evenly down the east wall. She is about to leave, making up her mind to come back the next day and begin an actual stakeout, determined now to follow through, when she sees a glass cupboard. She missed it the first time because it's unhelpfully placed on the same wall as the doors.

Reading through the building's tenants she finds what she's looking for sandwiched between an advertising firm and an architect, buried at the end of that ubiquitous haiku of law firms: Krieger, Demesier & Exit.

Migod, she thinks. It *is* Frank Exit.

FRANK.

She makes her way back to her apartment, the thought no longer heard, but looped and fully occupying her mind as mantra noise. At her apartment door she fumbles with her keys in a rushed anxiety to be inside, but once there, the pile of papers—which she realizes is the totem she wants to see—is no longer an oasis of the real, and isn't helpful.

She spends a fitful night in front of her desk anyway, absentmindedly sketching stick-figured fat men and stick-figured thin men, an arrow between them designating the progression, labeled with a question mark.

The next morning, after a few hours of forced sleep, she decides to break her routine and head straight for the swimming pool.

She's never attended the pool's "early bird" lap hour. The crowd is even more anonymous than her afternoon's. Everyone's groggy eye is turned inward. She notes this but then her eye also turns inward, not groggy but ragged from the sleepless night. Her muscles protest as she brings her arms through the water, as her legs kick. The water smells more heavily of chlorine than usual, and surprisingly the crowd is heavier, so Sarah is sharing her lane with someone. Frank Exit probably, but goggles and hair glued inside a skullcap make the man anonymous.

She imagines her lane sharer really is Frank, and gives him a head start and then thrashes through the water to catch up to him, staring through her goggles, across the wavy blue, focusing on his kicking feet and pulling hard to reach him. She repeats this chase for three laps, before the guy gives her a hard stare and waits for her to swim ahead. Embarrassed, she creates the acceptable distance between them. They become synced: she reaching a wall while he reaches the opposite. Turn. They are closest in the middle of the pool, as they pass, their white thrash and wake become the only contact now between them. As she settles into her pace, she thinks, *Why not? I'll go see Frank.*

When she and Jim had returned to the States, Jim had introduced her to Frank—her husband's oldest and best friend. She had been completely undone by his fatness that first meeting. Jim, of course, hadn't mentioned it, and she was shocked at how deep her bigotry went.

She hated fat people. She didn't know where this prejudice came from, but it was consistent and entire in her. She viewed their sexual being as helplessly pitiable—lecherous, desperate, and powerless. She had spent that whole first meeting staring at Frank's belly popping out of his tucked-in shirt.

The one time he had appeared with some dignity was at their wedding. Jim had asked Frank to be his best man. She did nothing to sabotage this, and fought consciously to bury her repulsion. Her discrimination was sinful, she knew, and she made every attempt to hide its existence from others. Deep down, however, she knew it was hopeless. She would always hate fat people.

At the wedding, however, she saw Frank for the first time with something resembling respect. Frank was comfortable and proud in his role at the wedding. He was wearing a well-cut suit and she could think of him as stately, dignified.

It was the last nice thought she'd ever had about him, until today.

After the wedding, she dealt with Frank as civilly as possible, hiding from him all her hostility. Which wasn't hard because Frank went into a deep, self-absorbing funk. Still, it was a burden compromising her hate in this way, and it was an immense relief when, several years after their wedding, Frank moved to Philadelphia.

Frank's move, however, ruined her marriage. She had never thought so, until now, when she realized that Jim's obsession and frustration in not being able to help Frank transformed his little incompetencies into dysfunction. Nothing obvious, but his sulking about that loss never really ended, and the moldy atmosphere that grew around him became unbearable.

What finally capped it off was Jim's loss of contact with Frank. They had initially received letters, conscientiously spaced phone calls, which spoke of Frank's success as a lawyer, his unexpected prosperity, and—his unending depression.

Then, he dropped off the radar. The line had been disconnected and the letters came back. It was a mystery, but they were already very involved in their own lives, working to keep their marriage together. She hadn't realized until now that finding Frank might have been the one thing that could have saved it.

She grows angry. Her husband's mystery, the thing that broke them and could have saved them if he'd had the intelligence and will and heart to forget *or find* Frank is now transferred to her.

And the mystery is given to her via a package based on her own deep and hidden bias, for—and this is the shocker: Frank is thin.

SHE'S WAITING OUTSIDE HIS OFFICE, hidden in a shaft of shadow, waiting and watching for Frank. When he comes out of the building and gets in a cab, she doesn't even think about it, just hails one herself and finds the cliché in her brain's repository of culture, laughably appropriate: "Follow that car."

He heads further uptown, and she is nearly distracted by the feeling of being in a cab, seeing the city through its windows. The movie game she'd made up, she realizes, must not be unique. Everyone must do the same, glorify their personal long pan up Third Avenue into the opening shot of the next Coming Attraction.

She gets out of the cab somewhere in the Upper East Side. He's gone into a building and, trying to look casual, she walks over to the door. There's a sign on it, and she recrosses the door three times in order to read it properly, more from nervousness than length of reading material. Uncool and self-conscious, she finally reads:

MADAME MADELEINE ELSTER,
PSYCHIC ADVISOR AND PARANORMAL.
BY APPOINTMENT ONLY. WALK-INS WELCOME.

She stops in front of the door, self-consciousness forgotten in the face of this advertised paradox, until—she hears someone coming.

She quickly crosses the street. Looking back she sees that it isn't Frank emerging from the building but a tastefully dressed woman with a bright, light-blue handbag. Not your assumed fortune-teller client, thinks Sarah, but then, how would I know? Not removing her eyes from the door more than necessary, she's fortunate enough to find a seat at a bagel shop across the street, which offers the appropriate view.

The woman with the blue purse returns. She wears a turquoise designer dress—simple, expensive spring clothing—and confidently pulls the psychic's door back and re-enters.

Curious, thinks Sarah, and for the first time the possibility arises to her that Frank's visit is not to the psychic, but to some other apartment in the four-story building. She sees Frank leave, and watches as he walks south, turns the corner and heads east on Eighty-Seventh Street.

She hesitates. Following Frank on foot seems risky. If Frank spots her, she knows she'd fumble the encounter. After all, *she* isn't disguised. If anything, she feels dramatically unchanged from the last time they'd met.

After some thinking, she decides to quit while she's ahead. At least, now, she can still follow out her original plan and just call on Frank tomorrow.

She throws away the cold dregs of her coffee and heads out of the bagel shop. A resurgence of curiosity however stops her from going to the subway. Instead, she crosses the street and walks into Madame Elster's.

The waiting room, for that's what it must be, seems an uncanny likeness to the waiting room of some tony group dental practice—at least this is how she would imagine it: a single leather sofa, Klee prints, and a selection of news and financial magazines splayed on a glass coffee table.

Sarah takes this all in as the ding of the electronic bell dies its lonely death in the room's hush. A voice fills the void with a May I help you?

Sarah looks up and is surprised to see a good-looking man. His gestures are graceful and he's got this action-hero charisma that she wouldn't think floors her, but it does.

Um, yes, do you have a . . . what are your prices? Sarah asks, collecting herself.

Surely, he says and hands Sarah a black binder, with the professionalism of a waiter bringing the wine list to the rabble.

Sarah glances through the binder, an unpleasant feeling at the sight of the incomprehensibly large numbers. She reads the notice at the bottom of the last page, *Madame Elster does not give stock advice,* and returns the binder to the receptionist with a Thank you.

I must have the wrong address . . . How do, do you know how to get to apartment 3C, she improvises.

Er, the receptionist's countenance breaks, and Sarah suddenly can see all his flaws, his imperfect pant line, a slightly too large freckle on his forearm. He's mortal, and she now envisions him a grad student, luckily working his way through a doctorate at an "interesting" job.

You must have, he continues, well, there's no, there isn't a 3C in the building. No, no, Ms. Elster lives upstairs and the, the office . . . we occupy the whole building.

She catches the update of Madame to Ms., shrugs a second awkward thanks, and leaves.

SHE'S WAITING OUTSIDE FRANK'S office building the following day—the not-quite-real notion she has is to "bump" into him on the street and thus avoid the awkwardness of a secretary's message.

She ends up just following him again. Another expensive taxi ride up. Frank leads them to a block just two south of Madam Elster's. He must live around here, concludes Sarah.

Frank heads into a bar and Sarah positions herself outside, on a bench located on the street's concrete divide. In the middle of the road, on what's usually reserved for naps by the homeless, she'd be conspicuous if anybody was bothering to look, but—no one is.

She takes out a travel guide—the only reading material she has on her—and fakes a study of fashionable restaurants in Lisbon.

Across the street, the woman with the blue handbag enters the bar.

Maybe Frank dates a psychic, she thinks, as the two come out of the bar. She thinks to follow them, but she sees them turn a corner, greet a doorman, and enter an apartment building.

Unmoved, hours later, still on the bench, she hasn't yet seen the woman or Frank leave. A general and insidious jealousy rises in her as if needed to counter the slow degree sink of the early summer evening. Not an anger at the woman whom she doesn't know, nor at Frank whom she thinks she knows well enough not to lust after, but the fact of a coupling, mutual and assumed consoling, somewhere occurring several flights above her.

—Stakeout?

—What? . . . Seated next to her, for how long she can only guess, is a bum. Homeless, unhoused, indigent. A Bartleby, a beggar, a bum. He's wearing a rancid black suit, which barely covers his portly frame, and which pinches whenever he makes the mistake of trying to gesture (as he does now, pointing to where Sarah's been staring).

—You've been sitting too long even for daydreaming. Must be watching someone I figure, or waiting to watch.

She can't understand how this much mass could have snuck up on her, not to mention the smell, which she realizes she's been inhaling for some time, now unfortunately all too conscious of.

—What are you looking for?

—No one, just. Nothing. I'm just sitting here . . . her sentence fades out of her mouth as if surprised at the strength it takes to speak, and immediately then, not bothering to.

The bum leaves. She is back in her reverie so that again she doesn't notice it. Staring still at the door the two had disappeared into, she's about to admit everything and point it out to the bum, but turning, she sees he's not there to confess to. Instead, she rises and heads to the bar where Frank and the psychic had met some hours before.

Investment bankers and hedge fund lawyers crowd the bar from dark wooded wall to dark wooded wall. It'll be spun off. You're untouchable now. And so the trial can't hurt it. It's a bargain. Utilities! Ha! We'll launch next week.

She orders a scotch. The amber drops like a solid ball into her empty stomach, then explodes in slow motion, a warmth tingling her scalp. She's instantly drunk.

She orders another, enjoys salting her wounds in a place like this. The ties loosened, the long brown hair thrown back as a throat is bared by a woman's proud laugh. Two men's heads bowed to each other, organizing a heroic financial attack with the moral assurance of chess grand masters. "Roads not taken" is the advertisement she reads chiseled into the glass of her fourth scotch.

Some time later, completely concentrating to maintain the pretension of sobriety, she calmly walks to the door, slightly off from the floor's perpendicular—her dignity intact!

Green globes of some subway in some direction are found. The painful impatient lean against a station pillar, waiting for the miracle of the train's arrival, which does come, finally, fueled, she thinks, by only the faith of the devout—hers—that it would.

In and out of consciousness, she stares out the window across from her, a mirror in between stations. She sees the psychic staring at her, adjusting some imperfection of blush with her finger, resettling the handbag on her lap. Later, another bum reclines on the seats across from her, opens one of the car's windows and screams FUCK! at the sudden echo of rush and machine which then enters. Hours or minutes later, he's gone and another comes over to close it.

When the train rises up again, somewhere in the Bronx, she's sober. She gets up to look at the map, figure out where she is and how to get home.

SHE STOPS AT HER APARTMENT only long enough to grab the things she needs for the pool. Her stomach is still empty and she feels poisoned, but her head seems remarkably clear. She makes the "early-bird" hour again, swims a few laps, and then gives up.

She grabs her knees and sinks a few feet into the water, looking across the pool's blue universe truncated into lanes. She keeps scanning the area between a black drain and the metal ladder that leads, it feels just now, to some unreal and unimaginable world.

The lifeguard squats by the water's edge and taps her. Startled, she splashes up and soaks him.

—Jesus, you shouldn't . . . sorry, but you can't do that, you're blocking the lane. You can warm up if you need to . . . over there, but it's, now it's too crowded here.

She nods, and the lifeguard shakes his head and walks away.

Afterward, she goes to a Chinese take-out restaurant and mechanically shovels into her mouth spoonfuls of chicken fried rice from a Styrofoam box. Back in her apartment, she lies in bed for a few hours before killing time in less painful ways, waiting for the hour Frank will leave his office.

Jim Fog and Judy Barton

JUDY HAD MOVED IN. They continued to sleep on the small mattress with its weak springs. Neither minded, though each thought the other did. Occasionally he would smell the house and think it dusty. She read on the couch in the morning before she went to her job at the library. The light would be very white then, and when he called to her from the kitchen, his voice was held and made more dense by echo. She was thinking about becoming a paramedic or a nurse. He wanted to continue teaching.

In spring they began to worry less about how comfortable they were getting with each other. A year passed so it was summer again. That determined it. The house began to receive their attentions.

She arrived home one evening and said she had got a desk. Some of her hair was sticking to her neck with sweat, and she asked for a glass of water as she sat next to the kitchen table. He was cooking dinner. A rhythm of slicing was on and at first he was only listening to the sound of the board and the knife he held in his hand, turning a few times and reflecting her smile. But then he heard her and could see she was excited, began to ask questions as best he could. A desk. Why? It turned out she hadn't actually bought it, but that the library was giving it away, and she had asked for it.

The weekend came and they borrowed a truck. They were told to come early, so as they drove through the town, most of the stores were closed and only a few people were out, running what errands could be done. Since it was summer, the lines of the town already were intersected and divided with yellow light and shadows. He was not yet awake and slightly uncomfortable in the hot cab of the truck. His back was wet though there was the breeze from the window across his legs. But that it was there, he didn't know why they were getting it, yet—since there involved little sacrifice, what was there to mind? She didn't know why also, but did imagine some use could come, which would recommend this moment's foresight.

Walking in, a man greeted them, whom Judy knew. They were guided to a corner in the back where it was—a large metal desk, looking heavy, but he understood immediately what she saw in it. Apart from mobility, it seemed perfect in function: broad, usefully sized drawers, a gravity and durability he guessed came from its institution, but an outdatedness that came immediately from nothing but the halt of its kind's production, decades earlier, which gave it the questionable (but they didn't) charm of unique possession.

It was heavy though. All three—the man helped—sweated the small distance to the truck. No need to strap it down I think, the man said. They laughed.

They placed it in the living room and throughout the weekend, though untouched, it was a pleasant surprise to either's crossing upon it.

On Monday he was left alone with it. He placed his cup and book on it and sat in the chair she had placed in front of it. Again he opened each drawer, which slid smoothly out and then back again, clicking shut. He felt childish and happy playing with the desk. There was too, he found, a comfort in the uprightness of the desk, the posture in the chair made him feel uncostumed in his reading. He spent the morning there, ate his lunch at it, on it, around it. Only in the afternoon, finding the day almost gone, did he leave it.

As he was preparing their dinner, he hadn't quite forgotten the morning, though did regularly wonder why he was feeling so well, so calm. She came home and went to the bathroom, washing out the day, transitioning, and her voice was slightly tired. He was placing the dishes down for dinner and, seeing her, was excited again. He spoke in rapid bursts through the door.

She smiled into the mirror and, rinsing her face, thought his excitement so much like a dog's, or a child's. Her baby. Coming out, kissing him, she asked if he had left the house. Yes, he said, sheepishly, realizing how he'd assaulted her. For cigarettes and the groceries.

They sat down to dinner. She told how a man had come in, the one, did he remember? who would only speak to her. Today he wanted to know about Genghis Kahn. She was laughing now. A lonely man, not too old, who had a fixation on horses and how one would use them in battle. It puzzles me, the man had said. I've never ridden, but how d'you suppose the fighting's *done*?

Jim told her what he'd read, a biography on an architect, and about a commercial he'd heard on the radio for a movie. They could see it maybe this weekend.

She washed the plates and he went to the other room, turned on some music, went out to the porch. The rough chords followed him there, dissolved through the house and yard. She came out to find him sitting, waiting. Why are our concerns so diffuse?

She compacted herself on the chair next to his. It's not that we're too late for ambition, she answered, but there's no compulsion for it. Maybe, he said, we just aren't.

It doesn't bother me. She turned her head.

Nor me, he said . . . neutrally, but was unsure. She had been in the theater, Jim knew. When he had asked, once, she had said, I'd been successful for thirty days in a circle of about that many people. He knew nothing about that, asked little, but did wonder what even that satisfaction was like.

Still, he said, I thought this summer I'd, maybe we'd, fix the house up.

Fine. Good. And she closed, briefly, one eye, putting her arm over the chair's arm, bringing her chin onto it. He had wanted for them to learn Russian too, and had signed up for a class but then—didn't go. The cartoon of it had lost its humor when she saw it a second, third, fourth time. But she accepted it, nauseating but innocuous, finally. He, of course, hated her if she admitted any doubt in him, then hated himself for what was true, came to look away when she mistimed her enthusiasm.

He lit a cigarette and thought himself calmer, absent-mindedly went inside to change the music. When he returned she had turned on the light and was reading. He sat and watched her, amused because she was nodding off. The lines of the book she was reading blurred and she felt in herself a sweet tiredness, a sleep she was fighting more out of play than need. Then she actually did dream. What was most important to her was him, and she thought, as she always thought, to tell him a secret, one that would bind them together or repulse them apart completely. Not having to, she never did. In her dream, she saw her father—tall, skinny, wearing the waiter's black suit he had worn the last time she had seen him, several years ago. Then she opened her eyes and saw that it was dark and the music had stopped. He was looking at her.

Maybe we'll go to some garage sales this weekend, he said. She smiled and got up, rolling her head around her shoulders to stretch. Are you coming up? and they walked up the stairs together.

Lying on top of their old mattress, they held hands and he turned his head toward her and told her about the desk and how he had passed the morning with it. She rolled to her side, her head on him, and placed her hand on his stomach. So that was it, she thought, and stroked his arm slower and slower until she stopped.

But it stuck; the details accumulated. He would sometimes spend a day, maybe a week, adjusting two or three pieces of furniture. She would be surprised but happy coming back to the home as she left it, or, how he had come to arrange it—either a careful gesture. They purchased moderately, arranged with a developing sense of balance.

Yet no need to make it forever, they both agreed, and so at some point soon after, all was done. The house was as it would be.

Oh but one thing remained. Couldn't he paint the house? She would help; that was how they'd met, she reminded him. Then the landlord was consulted and this introduced some consequence.

He wanted to sell the house—a decent price—as he wanted the money to retire and move. No hurry but think it over and sure, paint the house. They said they would think about it, but didn't just yet, for the immediate concern was painting. Or, they pushed it off as something to deal with at a more deliberate time. So that the painting became something of a party. Getting up one morning, feeling intelligent for picking the right clothes, they went to the hardware store to buy supplies.

Which color? It was a delight for her to decide, as it was for him to defer. She looked at the color charts, imagining the house, and felt it a wonderful responsibility. She chose a light blue and a slightly darker one for the shutters, pipes, edges. They drove back and, suddenly—they were at it. The smell of the vapor and their communion in space, circumscribing the house. The repeated regular sound and the human pace of a wall's covering. She thought perhaps this is why people love math, and turned to walk over to him, explain that, but then it seemed ridiculous, or, what was there to tell? he had his own expanding surface, his own silence and rhythm.

After a few hours, they stopped for lunch. Wordless still, they entered the house, confirmed with nothing less than a dramatic grope each other's suddenly present desire. Smiling, grateful, their bodies—free from the stiff positions of painting—released to lovemaking. After, content, resting on top of the sheets, they were slick, naked, paint speckled. Then a shower, and she made sandwiches while he looked through a magazine. They painted for a few hours more and until they went to sleep, it continued—an unarticulated and muscle-bound happiness.

A FEW MONTHS LATER IN FALL, as he is walking home from the school, he finds himself in a storm. It's a short distance to his house but he gets caught in it. At first it is almost exciting to be there, with the sky angry and powerful, wetted through with cold rain, knowing that soon there will be a yellow light in his bathroom and a warm shower. He stands in it, the noise of it all that he can think—leaves blown through, rained upon.

Then he has a sentimental thought about Judy, and—wants to see her immediately. He walks through the rain, thinking horrible scenarios of her death and his mourning of it. He knows his thoughts are outrageous and tries to stop thinking this way, but can't. He rushes the remaining distance home, but she isn't there yet. Of course, he realizes, she doesn't get out of work for some hours yet. But, home, all his anxiety seems foolish and he gives up even the idea of calling her.

Now he does go up, to the bathroom, strangely shadowy in the afternoon storm, and tugs on the chain that fills the room with anticipated yellow light. He strips and places his wet clothes in the sink and turns on the shower.

The steamy water covering him, wiping away his cold, he wonders why the storm had affected him this way. It reminds him for some nostalgic reason, of his mother, and now also, Judy. He thought he would propose marriage that night, but when he leaves the bathroom, when the cold air strikes him, the thought seems funny, unserious. Something has come over me, he thinks, I feel emotional and drained.

Another memory then. After his father left them, his mother had moved them to an apartment near the mall. They had lived there for only a year, but it was the closest that they had been, negotiating the small quarters, sharing a life, almost, he now thinks, though he might have been eight or nine then, almost like a man and wife. He thinks his mother, a tough woman, had reached the bottom of her life that year. They had been abandoned and he thinks now, that that was probably when she had given up, finally, and her death several years later was just its conclusion. But the time in that apartment, caring for each—how fragile they both were!—had been also a moment he tried to return to, in all his relationships. But it wasn't possible, he says to himself, each day its own.

He puts on fresh clothes and goes downstairs to make dinner. The blankness of the storm's noise and his nostalgia is broken by the din of her return. First it's the car's approach up the driveway, then when she opens the car door he hears the news on the radio spoken by a familiar voice, and then that ends, there's the door's bang and her running inside, shaking off, rustling out of her coat. She comes over to kiss him and look over the mail. Unlike him, she always appreciates this, is not made to see it by a rainstorm or a song or any other sentiment. She looks over their domestic habit with gratitude, always.

But when, at dinner, he tells her what he remembered, of his mother and the apartment by the mall—she knows that he had thought about her that day with some emotion. She hesitates before taking advantage of it, but she's found him an inconsistent man and thinks it would be the best for both of them if she, now, mentions the house. He may want to, but not realize until the house is owned—it's a dangerous assumption but, she loves him and wants it to work so takes the risk.

I've been thinking, she starts. We could take a loan, it's a good time.

He isn't surprised that she mentions it now. In fact he knows that the instigation is somehow his own. Not maybe when he began telling about his mother, but maybe at the end—he could feel, as he was talking, some movement of her head and the space opening up for her to make the demand. Let's call the bank and see what can be done, he says.

Satisfied, she tells him about her own day. The book all the children want to read. It's been reserved for months so she thinks maybe she'll organize a story hour for it. And other details, watery gossip, told over his chicken, over the bread. Afterward he goes into the other room while she cleans up.

Over the dishes, she plays a game, guessing what he is doing. She can picture him, moving through the other room, wavering over books, finally picking two or three and going out to the porch to wait for her. In a way, she has complete control over him, dominating and knowing him. But that he could surprise her and *not* be picking out books at all, but instead that he could go upstairs and clean the bathroom or decide to take a walk or watch television! He could do any of these things, and if so, she thinks, she wouldn't know him at all. She would only have imagined her power over him and he, without even intent, would have won a game he did not know he was playing. Her thrill at the possibility, this reversal and surprise, she reckons is the emotion of love—so she follows it, allows it, and thinks of it as a complicated gamble where she is risking everything for some ultimate happiness. In this way she justifies her manipulations of him—possibly correctly.

ON A SUNDAY MORNING, they were on the floor making love. She was on top of him looking down, riding him sweetly, intimately. Though she liked it, told herself she was into it, she had the premonition, almost a certainty, that she wouldn't come, that it wasn't right for it to happen. But as if reading her thoughts, he whispered to her, between his exertions, Is this good for you? Yes, she said. She felt then, in time's distance, an orgasm flying away like a piece of paper that had just blown from her hand. She knew she could run it down, fetch it, but there was an indignity to it—the work to get there, run after it and make a leap to finally step on it and have it. And not that she thought this, but that it was just something she knew, believed in by nature: everything was work. So she rode him, less sweetly now, with that specific ambition.

It was during sex that he did really love her. In that body to body union, part to part. In that making of love. It wasn't the groaning satisfaction of it, or not only that. Not that he felt accepted, not an absolution from his specific fears (that he was alone by race and temperament, abandoned, lacking vision, alone), but an integration of himself with the world. His solitude was, for those moments, finally nullified and a unit was created . . . with the world? of it? rather a world without, finally, a problem of identity. He was a nerve, skin. He forgot his name and became her belly button.

What does she feel at that moment? She thinks herself separate from him, doesn't really notice that he's there, save, vulgarly, what's necessary. She loves him least, though still, during sex. Yet for this difference, for these differences, they commune well in lovemaking, get what's needed from the other so feel symbiotic enough to think the act a success.

She rises from the floor, gathers her clothes, kisses him. He rolls over, reaches for the book he'd been reading, continues to read it. When she returns, freshly showered and dressed, he's still there, reading still, naked, lying on his stomach. She brings him a cup of coffee and he lazily rises and pulls on his pants.

Let's look at the house, she says. Alright.

He gets up and first they go outside to walk around it. He almost gets dizzy looking at its structure, Victorian style, with the awnings and the porch and its shape compact in a tight, static mix. The topology of the roof, for instance, though common enough, is one he can never get how conceived, a puzzle of space.

They continue inside, going through each of the rooms, watching themselves for any crisis of doubt. But it is too familiar for that, as if they had made it themselves, complete with their life together, inseparable from that new moment that he would recall beginning ecstatically but which did begin, like this, with common details accumulating.

At the end, in the attic, she looks around, memorizing the light, as if a scientist, to compare it with tomorrow, when they would sign the papers and own it, see if it stayed the same.

Sarah Car and Frank Exit

THE BUM SITS ON THE CONCRETE in front of the Citibank. He is fat, a mass of soiled black suit sweating in the summer sun and, from which, a single sound can be heard coupled with a single movement: he jingles a coffee cup. He's such an aberration of the success evident all around him that he's not noticed except for maybe the drop of change which only adds another (unheard) aural dimension to his jingling. A bum with a coffee cup.

Sarah Car is across the street, pacing in the block of shadow afforded to her by day's end and skyscraper. She's pacing, even though she doesn't want to, but—can't help it. She's just anxious to see Frank come out of his office building so she can follow him. Since spending the night on the subway, she hasn't slept much. She's lost that time. All she knows is that she sat in her apartment and watched the clock tick toward the hour she could come to Midtown for him, resume her following of Frank. Not that she thinks there's anything more to learn, just that it seems to her the only thing she can do. So she's lost that time, is not even completely sure how much time she did lose—a day? a week?—the time is just gone, the blank space between chapters. Her life is a succession of Meanwhiles and Hourslaters, punctuated by regular Nightfalls.

For now, she's only aware, only alive, when she's chasing Frank, though today she made provisions. She stops her pacing to take a drink from the thermos she's prepped. It is the only meal she's had that day: coffee, heavily fortified with vodka. The bum can't help himself and, from across the street where he's watching, licks his lips.

So there's another movement to the bum's sitting, aside from the cup-jingling, which the careful observer can see. The bum's eyes move slightly to and fro with Sarah's pacing, like a newscaster's eyes moving just noticeably as he reads the teletype above the camera.

But Sarah doesn't notice. That someone is following her with the fanatical self-involvement with which she is following Frank is absurd. Much of her mania is, in fact, due to the solitude of her task, that no one cares or is watching what she's doing, as embarrassing or even illicit as it may be.

So when Frank does come out of the office building, when a muscle in her neck tenses involuntarily, when she stops pacing and begins following Frank, she doesn't notice at all that the bum rises also, pockets the change in some cavernous pocket inside himself, tosses his now-empty coffee cup, and follows her.

Frank's feeling a touch nervous about his destination, not that he has reason to think anybody's following him, but such a destination breeds a certain anxiety. As much How will he perform? as Is anybody watching?

But he's done this so many times before that the anxiety is rote, and he doesn't look over his shoulder. Not once. So that Sarah's job is pretty easy. Just keep him in reasonable sight. The afterwork rush is heavy and she can just blend into the crowd. She's a little curious that Frank doesn't get in a cab today and instead is walking. But it's a beautiful day so maybe Frank is walking home, except they're going south. She pretends to look at jogging suits on sale while Frank scans newspaper headlines in front of a deli.

The bum's job is more difficult. First of all he's definitely more conspicuous, no matter Sarah also doesn't look over her shoulder. She would spot him immediately if she did happen to turn around and she'd remember. If she saw him twice, she'd know. Secondly, though the pace of the trio is set by Frank, the bum is fat and he's not used to it even if Frank and Sarah both consider it leisurely. Finally, the bum is sick and dying. He's got pancreatic cancer. And though he doesn't know it by that name, he knows that sometimes the jingling isn't on purpose but by spasm and that sometimes the pain makes it wrenchingly difficult to get to the flophouse where he rents a cot. So he's working the hardest, of the three.

WHEN FRANK GETS CAUGHT at a light, when the traffic makes him wait at the corner, Sarah, at first, dallies by a pay phone, in order to not get too close. But as the walk continues south, past Union Square now, and into the East Village, she's starting to get more confident. She's starting to even enjoy how completely hidden she is, so that she gets closer and closer to Frank. At certain times, she's standing right behind him, inches behind him in fact. Just another pedestrian waiting to cross, but close enough to see the cross-stitch in Frank's suit. The proximity makes her breathing shallow and the blood rush in her ears. The risk of being so close is an enthusiasm in itself, not in a perverted, stalking type way, or not only—but more childlike: the feeling of getting away with something.

In contrast, when either Sarah or the bum gets stopped by traffic, it's hell for the bum. He's huffing as it is and making all kinds of paranoid ducking movements whenever Sarah so much as scratches herself. Plus when he has to wait at a light, there's the anxiety of waiting and the feeling that she's getting away, and then he'll have to walk even more painfully *quicker.* So that, when he does get stuck behind a light, when he's standing in the group of pedestrians waiting for the WALK sign, there's the peculiar sight of him, the bum, kind of jogging his leg in impatience and even more strange, if he's getting real anxious, he'll actually jump to get a better view. The other pedestrians don't pay him much mind, just a stare as the fat bum (who smells bad, frankly) takes a kind of stunted, uncontrolled leap into the crowd, and they give him a little room.

As they get further into the East Village, the streets are a little less crowded, especially when Frank turns off of an avenue and onto a street. Here, Sarah slows down a bit and makes more space between herself and Frank, not only because the crowd is less but also because she senses Frank is near his destination. She starts to tense up a bit, in anticipation. The bum now knows where they're going but is worn out by this point. He also falls back, but is a little more confident and has a better view of Sarah, there in the distance, up the street.

Frank enters a barber shop, and Sarah stops, thinks a moment, and then turns and retreats about fifty feet, crosses the street to a point slightly out of view of the barber's window. She just stands and waits.

Sarah's turn and retreat scares the hell out of the bum. He was just starting to get his confidence back when Sarah turned and headed right for him. He all but dives into some trash bins. But Sarah doesn't even notice. Panting, he turns and walks all the way to the end of the street and waits at the corner, watching Sarah watch the barber shop.

Oh is that all, thinks Sarah, disappointed. A nice day and Frank decides to get a haircut. The obviousness of it isn't so much as the sheer banality of it. She's unsure why she's following Frank, but does expect something inexplicable, at least something remotely shady, which will match the mysteries of her own life. Some elaborate secret which, not by uncovering but by simply existing, allows her to understand her life's problems are not easily solvable and that she is, in fact, doing a decent job against unfathomably large odds. But a haircut! Life is simple and her fuckups are entirely her own.

The bum's heart is beating fast. He's spasming now, and grabs a wall, fingernails scratching the brick's red surface. Stay calm, stay calm, he tells himself. Don't punk out now, you sumbitch. He coaches himself through the spasms and is somewhat ready when Sarah begins walking again.

Frank has come out and is now walking farther down the street. Evidently he hadn't gone in for a haircut, but just to buy something—gel or shampoo, something—which is evidently in the plastic bag he's now swinging gently as he walks. Though this is vaguely strange to Sarah—when she knew him, Frank was never particular about his appearance, let alone his hair goop—it's still fairly pedestrian as far as unsolved mysteries go. And she follows him, a little hopeful still that developments might appear before nightfall.

Off the northeast corner of Tompkins Square Park, Frank enters a nondescript apartment building.

THE LIGHT IS BEGINNING TO DIE. Sarah has a good sight line to the door, seated where she is, in the anonymous comfort of a park bench. This building piques Sarah's interest, having possibilities that the barber shop, by its obviousness, did not. So she can hope a bit for satisfaction. She's given little thought to the furnishings of Frank's apartment or the aggressive nonstatement she guesses costumes his office. Something assumed, predictable, about all Frank's locales thus far. Save this building, so typical and unremarkable, has, for this reason, the smear of the seedy for Sarah. A sweated or yeasty or bloody crime—some act taking place that requires a body excretion. She copies the address into the margins of her *Let's Go! Europe* and unscrews the white plastic thermos. Throughout the day she's done this, drinking before she left her own apartment and finishing half the thermos earlier, while she was pacing in front of Frank's office building. She's on a binge, yet systems still mostly go. A little stagger now, maybe, if she tried to get up off the bench too quickly, maybe a wave of nausea if she thinks about food—but her focus and problem still clear.

The bum is now also seated on a park bench, behind Sarah. The two benches face away from each other and the bum is not really sitting on the bench in a proper way, but more like kneeling—his shins on the seat part and his stomach propped against the back part of the bench, so that he looks like some grotesque caricature of a child sitting. He's psyching himself up for his approach.

Sarah thinks she has a dangerous but controlled relationship with alcohol. She always drinks alone, but then again, she does everything alone. She drinks usually every night, but seldom more than two or three glasses of scotch. But when she's in a panicky or anxious type of way, and has nothing really to do, she'll feed on it, live off liquor. So, she's rather comfortable with her self-destructive drinking—or at least familiar. Still, she does wonder if it *is* an alcoholic vision when she sees the bum from the night (week?) before waddle up to her bench.

"You again?" she says.

"Y-you remember . . . Good, you recognize me. I wasn't sure—"

"It wasn't . . . It was only yesterday . . . Right?"

"Something like . . . Listen, could I sit?"

She moves over making room but is annoyed. She'd been safe, anonymous, watching Frank. No one knew or cared. That was safe. Now this . . . she ignores him and focuses on the apartment door there, in the distance.

"Listen," he begins, "Listen—will you, Will you *look* at me!"

She turns toward him abruptly. The demand in his voice frightens her—what does he want from her?—then she's angry. "What do you want?"

"Listen, this is hard too—Well, no, stop turning away, look . . . Do you think you've seen me before?"

"I already said I remember. Last night. You came up to—"

"No, not last night. I mean before then. Before last night, had you ever seen me before?"

"No."

"Are you sure?"

"No, I already said no. What more . . . Look, I'm busy. Could you leave me alone?" Frustrated, she goes into her bag and takes out a cigarette. She continues looking across the street to the apartment building, trying to ignore him, but feels him staring at her. Glancing to him, she can see he is still staring at her, frustrated, but his eyes are hungrily, pathetically, following her cigarette. "Jesus, you want one? Do you smoke?" He nods and she gives him one, lighting a match for him.

Suddenly, he grabs her elbow, making her jump.

"Sorry—"

"Don't fucking touch me."

"Sorry! Just—"

"I'm serious."

"One more question."

"What?"

"The suit."

"What about it?"

"Do you recognize it?"

"It's the same thing you were wearing last night, right?"

"Yes."

"But you want to know before then? If I saw it before last night?"

"Yes."

"No. And it smells like shit."

"Look, you're following Mr. Exit, right?"

This gets her attention finally. He knows something obviously, is part of it, though she remembers just then that he had hinted at such knowledge the night before. She exhales word and smoke: "Yes."

"I knew it."

"How do you know Frank? Do you work for him?" she says.

"Is Frank Mr. Exit? I don't even know his first name tells you how much I know. No, I don't work for him. I mean, not really. You want me to tell you about it."

They both can feel it, a small weight shifts—he knows something she doesn't. "If it's short."

"You won't believe me."

"Try me."

"I've got amnesia."

"Bullshit."

"No. It's true."

"Loada crock."

"I don't remember anything. I woke up one day two years ago and—nothing. But I know I know Mr. Exit—Frank—that I do know. One day I saw him and bingo, he was familiar. Every day not one familiar face. Not one that I see and can say *I know that face,* but Exit's, his I knew I knew. But I didn't know exactly from where, and I've been following him too and in two years I've learned next to nothing. I didn't even know his first name. But the funny thing is I think he recognizes me! I mean I was keeping my distance, but I sat in front of his office and . . . and he's given me a signal that he recognizes me."

"You're psycho."

"It's true."

"But what does this have to do with me? Do I look familiar? Do you recognize me?"

"No."

"So, why—"

"But you're following Exit too. I've watched you. I saw you when you stopped in the middle of the sidewalk. About a week ago. When you saw him but he didn't see you. Right? And you watched him walk into his building. Right?"

"That was the first day."

"Your mouth was open and you looked like you wanted to say something to him but he didn't see you. Right?"

"Yes."

"And for the past week you've been following him. I've seen you following him, so, so, so I thought you might know something. Something about me."

"But I don't."

The bum sighs and then asks, "Then why are you following him?"

"He was my husband's, my ex-husband's best friend . . ."

The bum fell back into the bench. "So?"

"I don't know. Look. Frank's just different. He's completely different. He even *looks* different from when I knew him. I wanted to find out more before I talked to him." She takes out the thermos and takes a sip. She feels his eyes on her hands and doesn't even ask this time, just thrusts the thermos to him, says, "Here," and watches his whiskered lips mouth the plastic opening. "Go ahead," she says, telling him what it is, "finish it up."

At this, as the lucky medicine washes through him, he forgets himself and tips the tall thermos back an even steeper angle and glugs loudly, twice. After he finishes, he says, "I can help you."

"How?"

"Do you know what's in that building over there, the one Exit is in?"

"No. Do you?"

"Yes."

"Tell me."

"Maybe. I want something in exchange."

"What?"

"Ask Exit about me when you see him."

". . ."

"—"

"Why don't you—"

"I can't."

They sit in silence for a long time after that. The alcohol slows time for both of them. She is momently, every moment, about to give her consent to his request, but keeps pausing. Her mind begins to ramble to itself. The bum, too, seems to lose track of what they've been talking about. They both just stare at the apartment building Frank's in. They've almost forgotten why they're looking at it. The door to the building has just become some focal point, keeping them from the more awkward business of looking at each other. So it is a surprise to both of them when

"Look, he's coming out."

"Yes, that's him," she says excitedly. They watch him walk to the avenue and hail a cab.

"Aren't you going to follow him?" he asks.

"No, I'm . . . I'm drunk and tired . . . Aren't you?"

"Do you want to know what's in that building?"

"Yes," she has an idea, "Listen, I . . . Let me . . . let me buy you dinner. We'll compare notes."

"They won't let me into a restaurant."

". . ."

". . ."

"With me they will."

"No," he objects, "they won't."

"OK, how's this. I want to know about Frank. So how about I let you take a shower at my place. You clean up some. Then I buy you dinner. This'll be a one-time deal, understand. I'm not a Girl Scout. A shower and a meal—what do you say?"

"You want me to tell you what I know."

"Yes."

"And you'll ask him?"

"Yes."

". . ."

". . ."

"OK."

"Good. What's your name?"

"Mac."

"Mac what?"

"I don't know. Mac. Just Mac."

"OK, I'm Sarah."

THEY TAKE THE TRAIN TOGETHER. He smells. Shit-piss and people move away from them.

He has difficulty with the three flights to her apartment. On each landing, she waits for him to catch his breath. ("Ready Mac?" she'd smile. "Yeah.") And then supports his arm and walks up with him.

She gives him a clean towel, leads him to the bathroom, and tells him to take his time.

When she hears the twist of the knob and the splurge of running water, she decides to get him some clothes. She runs out and buys a razor, a toothbrush, some underwear, socks, sweatpants, and a T-shirt.

When she comes back to the apartment the water has stopped running and she is worried he has left. She knocks on the door and, when no one answers, she enters.

He's asleep. He seems to take up the whole tub, his hairy stomach protrudes from the soapy water like a troll island. The bathroom stinks with his soiled clothes. His head is a swarm of wet hair and gray beard. She goes and gets a trash bag and stuffs his old clothes into it, thinks to throw them out, but changes her mind and leaves the sealed bag in the bathroom. She places the toothbrush, razor, and clothes on the sink and closes the door.

When it is all done, he comes out with the trash bag in his hand. She can see behind him and notes that he has conscientiously folded her towel and cleaned up the bathroom.

She appreciates this because she knows maneuvering in the small room must have been difficult for him.

He doesn't say anything but sees where she's looking. He's glad she notes his effort, which has cost him energy and willpower, but he'd persevered in order to send the message that he isn't just using her and is grateful.

Then she looks at him. The transformation's radical, as she'd expected. The neon-orange sweatpants give him away, but he almost looks like a citizen. His face, newly shaven, is gaunter then his oversized frame would suggest. His hair, wet and slicked back, reveals an intelligent forehead. "Where do you want to eat?" she says.

"What should I do with this?" he asks, lifting up the trash bag.

"You can bring it with you, or if you want, leave it here." She sees him hesitate. "I'll come up and bring them down to you. You won't have to climb the stairs again."

"No, it isn't that . . . OK," and he drops them in the corner.

"So where to?"

"I don't know. You decide."

"A diner? Something fancy? How about a nice fat steak?" she laughs cruelly.

"Someplace with booze."

SHE WALKS HIM DOWN THE STAIRS AGAIN. It's a slow procedure and she feels her hand is tiny and frail as it grasps his big, now exposed, elbow. Yet she controls him, and has become, somehow, immediately, his master. Again, they pause on each landing. She's sobering up now and in the silence of the stairwell, as he rests, she feels ashamed at the situation she's created. A guilt at being so powerful so easily.

SHE TAKES HIM TO A DINER, impressively new and ugly. The walls are tiled and colored and she feels like she's in an obscenely posh bathroom. It's garish, but Mac blends in well, she thinks, though wonders if that matters to him. There is a wall of glassed booze on display, and he seems satisfied.

He studies the menu and, when the waiter comes, asks for a ham sandwich and a double bourbon.

"That's all?" she asks him.

"I'm not sure if I can keep it down."

She orders a whiskey. After the waiter leaves, she asks, "Are you sick?"

He only warns, "I may order something, something else later."

The waiter returns with their drinks. They both sit silently and stare at them. A toast seems out of the question.

She picks hers up, takes a sip, and says, "Well, what do you remember?"

"I WOKE UP IN THE WOODS," he says. "I'm not even sure exactly where this was. Somewhere north. It was dusk, though at first I didn't realize this. I thought, naturally, that it was morning. I was very disoriented. This was about two years ago. I remembered almost nothing, though I did remember what I had dreamt about: crowds."

"Crowds?"

"Yes. I remember crowds, not huge stadiums but various-sized audiences watching something. I never knew what they were watching and it seemed to change. I mean the venue seemed to change, but always an audience of some kind, watching something."

"Was it you? Was it you they were watching?"

"No, somehow I was part of the audience too. I knew this, but I could never see what the rest of them were seeing. It didn't seem to be important anyway. Sometimes it seemed like a sporting event—a boxing match maybe. Sometimes an orchestra was playing, so it might have been a concert. I was part of the audience always, but, looking at the audience. The strangeness of this convinced me it was a dream and not a memory—so really I might not remember anything."

The waiter brings his sandwich. They both order another drink.

"SO I WOKE UP AT DUSK. Flat on my back, just remembering my dream, looking up and seeing the sky, my past completely gone. I was wearing the suit you saw me in. It was in much better shape then. I woke up, thinner, thin actually, in this suit, in a wood, flat on my back. It was dusk. I got up and walked around. It is an incredible feeling to wake up and not know why you are in a wood, to not know that it is actually dusk and not dawn, to not know your own name. Try it sometime. I found a small fire not far. It was at the end of a gravel road that came into the wood and stopped there. I followed the road out. By the time I came out of the woods the sun was below the horizon and it was getting dark quickly. I came out onto a highway. There were no cars. I stood next to the highway for a few minutes, mesmerized by the obvious and only choice I could possibly have to make: which way to follow the highway. Both stretched into the distance, their destinations as far as I could tell, identically meaningless to me. I was paralyzed from making a decision. Not a single car passed. I couldn't make up my mind so I went back into the woods and rebuilt the fire, which was easy since the coals were still hot, and sat next to it all night thinking nothing. In the morning I went back to the highway and tried again. I thought I'd go in whichever way it seemed like more cars were going. No cars came. Not a single one. I decided I'd go in whichever direction the first car that came along went. The whole day not a single car came by. I started to doubt my existence. It was easy to make the leap. You wake up without memory, flat on your back, and you begin to doubt. I lay down at the side of the road and fell asleep. I woke up with a start. I felt like I had just missed a car. I thought I could hear its rush still in my ear's memory. But when I looked—nothing. I looked one way and then the other. Nothing. The world had died and I was alone on it. I felt. You think to yourself, Just start walking. It doesn't matter which way, just choose and go. One foot in front of the other. But I couldn't. I was hungry and my mind was exploding from the crazy gulf that I had woken with, but I still couldn't move. One strange thing about that suit. When I woke up I was much thinner than I am now. I don't know exactly why but I've gained a lot of weight in the past two years. And I've worn that suit every day since the day I woke up. And it has always fit. It took me a long time to actually realize this. At first I didn't even realize I was gaining weight. Or it wasn't important to me that I was. But at some point I realized that I was much larger than I had been and that the suit still fit. As soon as I realized this, I never took the suit off. Today's the first day in a long time. I knew that I was meant to wear it. Perhaps someone would recognize me based on it, perhaps this was the only way they would recognize me and they had created this magical, biblical suit specifically for the purpose. I'm not sure. I may be crazy. It is a possibility I cannot escape. I may be completely nutsoid. On the third day, a car came up."

He takes a bite from his sandwich. Sarah sips her whiskey and waits for him to finish chewing.

"The car came up from the horizon and I just watched it come. First, in disbelief, then in amazement. What was amazing was not just that there was a car, but that it seemed to be slowing down. And sure enough, it stopped right in front of me."

IT WAS A BLUE CAR, newish. A Honda Accord, I think. The windows were definitely power windows. I remember them coming down smoothly. The veil to life falling, if you believe the state I was in. A woman was in the driver's seat. Your age, about. Straight brown hair. She leaned over the passenger's side and said, "Mac, wanna ride?"

I nodded, walked over, and got into the car.

"Where you going?" she asked.

"Where are you headed?"

"New York City."

"How far's that?"

"An hour and a half. Two hours."

"I'll go there, if you don't mind."

Pretty soon the road was full of cars and the landscape was housed and busy. I didn't even notice that it happened. Just realized, at some moment, that they were there. I thought to ask: "Where did you pick me up?"

"What do you mean?"

"I mean what was the closest town, do you think, when you picked me up?"

"Have no idea. I'd been driving for awhile. Hartford maybe. Don't remember. Say, Mac, what's your name?"

"You can call me Mac."

"Suit yourself. Mine's Judy."

We got into Manhattan. It was a strange feeling. Driving down the FDR, I recognized some things but not very clearly. I realized I'd been here before but also that it wasn't *home*—at least landmarks and smells did not jump out in familiarity, saying I'd spent much time there.

"Anyplace special?" she asked.

"Wherever's convenient."

She dropped me off in the West Village. Before I got out of the car she said, "Do you have anyplace to go?" I said that I didn't.

She said, "I'm having this party tonight. You can come and if you don't have any place to stay, I can put you up." And then she took out a twenty-dollar bill and wrote an address on it. She handed it to me. I didn't even realize how kind she was being. I mean I looked like a mess—better than when you first met me, but a mess. Two nights I had just spent in the woods. I took the twenty, put it in my pocket, and said, "Thanks." I got out of the car and watched her turn the corner.

I was hungry. I hadn't eaten in at least two days. So I went up to a hot dog vendor and bought three dogs with everything and a Coke. I wasn't thinking. I gobbled up the hot dogs and started to wander around drinking the Coke. I walked for hours but then I started to feel sick from gobbling up the hot dogs on an empty stomach. I finally puked on the sidewalk. After that I felt a little better and then it hit me. I'd given away the twenty. So I ran back to the corner where I'd bought the hot dogs, but—he was gone.

•

SARAH FINISHES HER DRINK. The waiter comes and Mac tells him to take away his half-eaten sandwich and to bring him another bourbon. Sarah asks for another whiskey.

"So what did you do then?"

"What could I do? I had no ID on me and less than twenty dollars. And no party to go to."

"Did you try the police?"

"Sure. It was the first thing that I did, but I knew nothing, remembered nothing, and already looked bad and was starting to smell. What were they going to do? Kick me out, that's all. They took a statement, but pretty much I was booted out of there after a little runaround."

"Then what?"

"Everything and nothing. Eventually I took to begging. It was the only thing left. I met some people and they taught me how to survive, but that was all. I survived. It's been two years, but I've been lucky in one way."

"How's that?"

"I started begging in Midtown. And on the very first day I spot Mr. Exit. I see your Frank coming out of the office building. He doesn't see me but I see him. And there's the spasm of recognition. I know him. I mean I *know* him!

"So I decide to jingle for change in front of his building. And the next day, the very next day! he sees me and gives me a twenty!"

"Just like the lady who picked you up."

"Exactly. And every week he's given me a twenty. And every week I pore over it, thinking it'll have a message, some clue to why this happened, but—it never does."

"Have you ever talked to him?"

"Once, when he was giving me the twenty, I looked up at him and asked if I looked familiar to him. I was worried because I thought it might freak him out and he wouldn't give me any more money. But he just kinda looked surprised and said, 'No,' and walked away. He's still given me a twenty though, every week."

"So you've already asked him. Why do you want me to do it again?"

"I don't know. Just for confirmation. He might have answered too quickly and might have remembered something later."

"Don't you think he would have told you?"

"Maybe, but maybe he doesn't want to for some reason. So if you asked him, if someone else asks him, it's a long shot but what else do I have. Maybe he'd tell you something."

"OK, I'll do it, but what else have you learned about him. You said you've followed him and that you've learned nothing, but I don't believe you. You've got to know *some*thing."

He stops the waiter and asks for another round. "Well yeah. I do know one or two other things. He's a lawyer, I don't know what kind but he's doing well. He doesn't seem to have a very active social life, but does do two things regularly. He sees that psychic lady, Madame Elster, every Thursday, and he goes to that building next to the park every Wednesday."

"What's in that building?"

"A brothel. An upscale brothel."

"How do you know?"

"I know. I've watched the people come and go."

THEY HAVE ONE MORE DRINK in silence. After it's done, he says, "Well, that's all I can tell you. I guess I should thank you."

"It's OK."

"You'll ask him about me?"

"Yes."

Sarah pays the bill and they walk back to her apartment. They are both drunk again, though she notices he's handling it better, or at least he is steadier.

He seems relaxed now, as if telling his story was all he needed to do. She smiles at him, happy now also. She thinks their small negotiations may pass for friendship.

In front of the building she says, “Wait here. I’ll go up and get your stuff.”

When she comes back down, he’s gone.

Jim and Judy

◉ ◉ ◉ ◉ ◉ ◉ ◉ ◉ ◉ ◉

YESTERDAY HAD BEEN A SUNDAY, the day after New Year's, and they'd gone out to see a movie. It had affected them and they'd walked slowly and silently back to the car. Even once in the car, as they waited for it to heat up, they didn't say much. The movie was a simple one, not particularly good or bad, but sufficient, if allowed, to move them.

At some point she decided the car was warmed up and put it in gear. He automatically turned on the radio.

Once home, he asked, "Do you want a drink?"

She declined and went upstairs to get ready for bed. She'd have to get up early in the morning. Not really early, but—at the normal time. In the kitchen, by himself, he sipped a beer and felt slightly guilty.

When he came into the room, she was already in bed but not yet asleep. He washed up quickly and joined her.

"How was day two?" he asked. She had decided to give up smoking.

"OK."

"You think you'll make it this time?"

"We'll see," she said.

Tomorrow would be Monday and Judy would have to go to work. Jim still had a week of his winter vacation left.

She had looked bleary in the morning, while he'd felt renewed. He thought, She's going to work today and I'm not and that makes all the difference.

He was slightly annoyed at her while she puttered around with her coffee. He wanted to start his day and he couldn't until she'd left. Then just like that, he was alone.

He was remorseful for about ten minutes as he did the breakfast dishes, but soon focused on all he could do that day. He was already caught up with all his school chores and was completely ready with lessons for next week. He thought he might write a letter in the morning, lunch, and then read his novel. Then in the afternoon he could go grocery shopping and fix the pantry closet. Then he'd cook something nice for dinner, something Judy would like. What would that be? He had the whole day to decide.

The letter was one that he'd been meaning to write for a long time. He knew it would be difficult, but he thought he would take a stab at it and then he'd read it over tomorrow, or in a week, and see if it was still worth sending out. That's how he dealt with letters these days.

This letter was to his ex-wife. He thought she was living in New York City and he had an address for her there, but it was more than two years old. How could they have lost touch so easily? He wanted to know if she was happy or not. And he wanted her to know that he was, now, happy. Not to gloat, but because he knew she'd want to know, would find comfort in knowing, if she herself was unhappy. She'd always been generous in this way.

Or she could be married. Maybe even have kids! That would have been impossible before, but now? And she might even be happier, better off somehow, than he was. Would he be equally as comforted? Probably not. He *wasn't* generous in that way.

He started the letter several times. He tried to give it a style she could recognize as his, but he had forgotten how he once was. He tried to convey his present self, but the words felt false. He tried to keep it simple and to stick only to the facts, but that too felt contrived. At the end of an hour he had grown frustrated and cross. He rose to make another pot of coffee and promised himself one more hour on the letter, but while in the kitchen, he got distracted with the pantry he was supposed to fix and forgot about the letter until much later.

Judy had asked him to fix the pantry a long time ago. It wasn't so much that it needed fixing, but what they called the "pantry" was a large walk-in closet between the kitchen and the garage. Jim had used it as a storage space ever since he first moved into the house, so that now it was filled with whatever junk he'd been too lazy to throw out or organize. Judy had been on him to clean it out for months. She thought they could put decent shelves into it and redeem the room back into the old-style country pantry it surely once was. Jim had his doubts.

Halfway through with emptying it, Jim became depressed. He had found a suitcase of old sweaters and a bicycle he'd forgotten about, things he had bought and kept from his first marriage and from his past travels. Jim really wasn't a pack rat; he threw away as much as he could, but here in that closet was everything he had been caught careless enough to have kept. What use could these old things have in his new life? But how could he preserve them?

He sat at the kitchen table growing agitated, surrounded by plastic trinkets and dusty lamps and broken hats, resting his legs on the back of the bicycle.

Then something happened as he sat there. If he thought about it—why he was mad at Judy—it would have struck him as absurd. But he didn't think about it. He just began, slowly at first, then totally, to be annoyed. Judy had made this happen. It was Judy's fault.

◉ ◉ ◉ ◉ ◉ ◉ ◉ ◉ ◉

IMMEDIATELY IF ONE OF THEM needed to have sex more than the other, power would be won by the other. Immediately. Neither wanted the power. Neither wanted to want so extremely that such power could germinate.

This was not unique for them now. Everything was calculated. Hurts remembered stopped the escalation of play into passions. They could even sense this, and tried to replicate danger or, sometimes, to actually let go, contact it, and remember by a smaller proxy pain, larger deeper and darker ones. This happened relatively quickly. It had been three years now since they'd bought the house.

But they also felt young still. Possibilities were not infinite, but surely some remained. A camping trip was one such small example. A few times it had come up but they hadn't gone. But this time, late summer, he'd suddenly thought, Why not? Not that he or she had much experience camping, just that on the horizon of the town, in bright green spots within it, they could see nature, which they knew nothing about except that it was pretty. So why not? She thought it was a good idea so took a Monday off and they made preparations for the long weekend.

They set off in the early morning. Once on the highway, he carefully poured two cups of hot coffee.

The night before he had been excited. Had it been that long since they'd gone anywhere? But now, watching as the dark grasses swept past them, he was subdued. The weekend already felt concluded, unknowns weren't so, or, he wasn't curious about them anymore.

But the sun did come, and the familiar radio station dissolved in a cloak of static, and things did seem new. She scanned the dial and though he feared she'd find the news again, and would then have to sit through it for another hour, she found music. Different music, sweet for being different, and crisp in the morning airwaves.

The clean car, the smooth length of road, the sealed and then released aroma of coffee. She felt as if all of humanity's progress had been made so that she could feel clean and new and efficient, traveling down the highway. He felt it too, and so there was this one unique hour, the second hour of their two-hour drive, which was peaceful and renewing.

The campground was crowded and, foolishly, they hadn't expected it. As they walked through it, the discovered necessity of small talk easily shattered the illusion of being apart from the world. It made him grumpy, and though he tried to pretend otherwise, he quickly became visibly miserable. She was annoyed at how fragile his expectations were, but—wasn't surprised.

Let's go for that hike now, she said.

Wait. I want to just sit here for a moment and smoke a cigarette.

She watched him waste another hour then, puttering around the campground. And when she'd almost given up on the idea of a hike, and had even lain down in the tent for a nap, he said, OK, let's go.

The trail went through the wood and bordered sharp beautiful cliffs. She wasn't looking at the scenery. She was too annoyed and, seeing this, though about to give up his crankiness, he soured back into it.

◉ ◉ ◉ ◉ ◉ ◉ ◉ ◉

THEY EXECUTED SO QUICKLY upon formulating their desire, were both so greedy about what could happen, thinking how it was such a sexually mature adventure, that their disappointment was particularly painful, rose-pink as it was, with embarrassment.

As far as he could tell, it was only a coincidence, but both Bill and Judy brought up the idea on the same day, though, granted, in different terms. With Bill it seemed a breathless possibility that he'd been nurturing for years, as if his entire slow-moving nonaccomplishment was actually hiding this precise, furiously worked-upon ambition. He said that Nancy had agreed, was into the idea as much as he was. They'd never have gone if he wasn't fully confident that they both felt the same way, he said. And the club, up in Columbus, was a couples-only affair.

Judy, that evening, spoke in general terms of the same thing. That they should experiment, maybe "open up" their relationship. "You've been talking to Bill and Nancy," he said, assuming that this was where she got the idea. But no, she said, she'd just been thinking about it and was wondering what he thought. Such was her surprise at linking the idea with Bill and Nancy that he believed that the two had, unlikely as it was, hit upon the idea separately but simultaneously. Like Leibniz and Newton.

◉ ◉ ◉ ◉ ◉ ◉ ◉

STILL: ONE EVENING AFTER DINNER, she joined him on the back porch. They sat and quietly mentioned one person, then another. One word was said and that was a very funny joke. And also, when they were running an errand on the other side of town, a large field with a farmhouse set in a distant corner that both of them had noticed, despite an argument. Also a man's glasses that both thought looked good, and maybe would also, on the other. And also he remembered that she had liked once how someone had cooked mushrooms, and asked if she had remembered it, and she said she did, and he said that on the phone that day, he'd spoken to the person and gotten the recipe.

◉ ◉ ◉ ◉ ◉ ◉

THEY WERE SCARED OF THE TOPIC, but both said that they didn't want children. And it turned out, eventually, that both meant it.

But one time, when he had brought it up, it led (strangely she had thought afterward) back to previous conversations that they thought they'd been done with.

"Were you happy in the theater?" he asked.

"Well, it wasn't really theater, but, yes, I was. For a moment, it sounds untruthful, but, well, it was the happiest time I can imagine."

"You were a director?"

"Yes."

"So why did you leave it?"

"I don't know. It was too hard to continue maybe."

He didn't believe her, but could never find reason to push further but did add, that night, "Isn't that where you said you met Frank?"

"Well, I knew him before that but that was how I got to know him better. He was like well he was a big fan."

"He liked your plays?"

"They weren't, more like performance art."

"Which you . . . directed?"

"Yes, but they were more like, they were parties."

"Parties?"

"Yes, you could say . . . Listen Jim, do you, do you remember your father very well?"

"Where'd that come from?"

"No, nowhere, but I mean, we were talking about whether to have children, so I thought—"

"Oh, well, I've told you. He left us. He left my mother and me."

"You don't remember him at all?"

"No, not really. I remember a trick he played with a tin can though. My only memory. He would, this was my step-father really, and he would—"

"What? This wasn't your father."

"No. I think, it's funny, well I've never really spoken of this. I don't know why . . . I can't be completely sure, but my mother told me, one time, a long time ago. I must have been, well I was very young. She had been crying, and she looked up and she told me a story about another man, a man in Korea who'd taken her once to a movie . . . he was a handsome man, she had said . . . and somehow, I was very young, somehow I got the impression . . . she, she told me that that was my father. We never talked about this again, and it's a strange memory for me, very precise and yet cloudy, and I can't be absolutely sure I'm not making it up. But, you know it's funny I'm telling you now. I've never told anyone, I think, except Frank. I didn't I didn't even tell my first wife, well, I think I tried, but things like that never, Sarah was never interested in things like that, believe it or not."

"Hm, you know from everything you've told me I always thought our fathers were similar but—"

"What did I tell you? I never said—"

"But maybe they were, but not as similar as I thought," a wave of relief went through her as she admitted, "my father was, he actually, he knew Frank and—"

"Really? You never told me that."

"They met once; they were supposed to meet again, at my last party, but he never came . . . My dad went a little crazy. He was a Southerner too, served in Korea too, and well, he had a bad time I guess. He would get strange ideas, always talking about flying outside his body, that his soul was corrupt and needed redemption, crazy talk. And he was an alcoholic. He'd get violent and mean."

"Did he ever hit you?"

"No, but he hit my mother. I remember it."

"And this is why you don't want children?"

"No, it's not that. Maybe it is I'm not sure and who knows. I'm not saying I won't change my mind, but—I can't see what would. No, I don't want them."

◉ ◉ ◉ ◉ ◉

THEY SPENT THE WHOLE DAY AT IT. They woke up on Saturday at the same time. She woke up from a dream that she couldn't remember but which had made her very wet and so she scissored her leg over him. He woke with a hard-on also, so there was a wordless initiation to it. She kissed his cheek so he opened his eyes and almost laughed, so obvious it was what they were going to do. She kissed his eyes and forehead and then kissed his chest and nipples, avoiding his mouth just yet for the embarrassment of her own's sour taste. He had lost his erection for some reason in the moment right after waking, but a cupping of her hand made it return.

Since she felt like, had in fact, made the first movements, he let her continue with them down past his stomach, now licking the head of his cock. She pooled spit in her mouth and wet her hand and stroked him.

After a moment he put his hands underneath her armpits and gently pulled her up and rolled her onto her back. He kissed and tongued her neck and then kissed her mouth. The morning dryness and sourness was quickly washed out by their tongues and spit and he could taste, past them, neither pleasant nor unpleasant, the smell from his cock, now in her mouth. He kissed and licked one of her nipples, flicking gently the other. Then still licking a nipple, he brought one hand down, tracing a line over her stomach to her cunt, and gently circled her clit.

Though it was more or less how they always started, he never thought, as she only sometimes did, that it needed more variation. Eventually she wanted him inside her and he squatted between her legs and teased her with the tip of his cock, went down to lick her pussy some, and then came back up and gently put himself inside her.

He didn't know how long he would be able to last. Sometimes, if he was still groggy in the morning and she was into it, he could continue for some time like this and make her come. But usually he came quickly this way so, after a while, after thrusting gently and then harder and then gently again and licking her breasts and sucking her fingers and having his fingers sucked, he rolled over and pulled her on top of him. He could last longer in this position and she liked how he grabbed and pressed her breasts together, biting gently and licking her nipples. She knew he was worried about how long he'd last and so took him at his word when he said, "Slower, slower." She told him to hold her ass and he cupped his hands around her cheeks, sometimes pinching them, occasionally slapping them which he still wasn't sure if she really liked. They came together and he was relieved and she was happy. "Good morning," she said and slid off to rest her head on his arm.

They didn't really have anything to do that day. After they showered together, they had a simple breakfast of cereal and toast. Her hair was still wet, though she had dressed while he was still wearing the sweat pants he had slept in. He still wanted to, and so as she was looking at the paper, came up behind her and put his hand down her shirt. She smiled and with one hand felt his forearm and with the other hand, reached back to feel his cock through his pants. They made love on the chair, which was harder for her and easier for him. It was harder on her legs but she could feel him, if not deeper, then in different places inside of her so liked it. He thought of suggesting getting the vibrator but knew she didn't like to use it while they were having sex, so, though it excited him, decided not to. He came and she didn't. He was looking directly into her eyes when he came and then immediately shut them, both for the emotion of release and because their gaze was somehow embarrassing.

She stood up off of him and he got on his knees and licked her to orgasm, seeing his own come drip down her leg and tasting it as well as smelling and tasting the soap from her recent shower. After this, they held each other on the couch and then drank coffee and read the newspaper. After a while, they turned on the television and watched it for a few hours, talking and joking.

She said she was hungry. But they hadn't *done* anything yet, he said, not really complaining. They went out and had lunch and, while having lunch, decided to see a movie. Afterward, they came home and they both wanted to again, though mostly because they didn't know what else to do. This time she suggested he fuck her ass, which she sometimes liked and he didn't so much but always agreed to. He bent her over the couch and licked from her pussy to her asshole, getting both wet. He eased her asshole open with a finger and with his other hand played with her hanging breasts. Then he fucked her pussy for a little while, pulling on her shoulders. Then he, gently at first, eased his cock into her asshole. Is that OK? he asked. She said it was. Do you like it? he asked. Yes, do you? she said. Yes, he said. He fucked her in the ass for a while and when she said to do it a little harder, he did. It hurt her and she sometimes but not always liked the pain. After a while she told him to lie on the bed. She spit into her palm and started jacking him off while biting and pinching his nipples. He convulsed and came hard. Afterward they napped.

When they awoke it was dark. They got up and she felt feverish and sated and slightly nauseated. She looked at him and laughed and said out loud, "Too much fucking!"

◉ ◉ ◉ ◉

A FRIEND OF JUDY'S HAD DIED. Someone she knew well once, but hadn't known very well recently. He had had severe diabetes and was the husband of one of her girlfriends. He had died at thirty-eight. She was surprised at how she didn't react to the news. It was a shock for someone of her generation to already be dead, but what could she say about it and what could she think.

Jim drove her to the airport. She was flying to Boston for a week to be with her friend. She didn't think she would be a burden and would even be of some help to her friend, so that was why she was staying for the whole week. As they were driving up, before chiding the selfishness in it, Jim thought how many people would ever get such a use from him.

At the gate they spoke about other things for a while. Bill's recent heart surgery. Nancy's level-headedness. The two were their best friends but, recently, they had also become something like parents to them. Older people that they took cues from, or whose example they studied and tried to correct if they thought they could. Many of their discussions led to them, and they expected that Bill and Nancy also often talked of them. The surgery was scary, but supposedly everything was better now. They spoke of it until the boarding announcement, and then Judy kissed him and got on the plane.

During the drive back, Jim wondered if Judy missed having more friends their age. It wasn't that there weren't possibilities in the town, nor did they never hang out with other, younger people, but for the most part it was themselves and Bill and Nancy. Would seeing her friend make her think they were too isolated?

◉ ◉ ◉

THE THING THAT TRIGGERED the change was Judy's new boss at the library. Not too slowly, and very obviously, Judy began to hate her job. She was trapped, though. There weren't many options for work in the town.

Eventually, after a year, she did get a different job. It was in Columbus and she even started enjoying the hour-and-a-half commute, which she thought of as a calming, meditative practice. The year before she got the job, however, was a miserable one.

"She's such a bitch," Judy said, breaking the silence of their dinner.

"Your boss?" Jim guessed easily. The same theme had been repeating for months.

"Who else."

"What happened this time."

"I don't want to talk about it."

"OK."

"She's already taken away all the money for the after-school programs and now she's told the other clerks they can't help me on the lessons. For no real reason. She says it takes away from their other duties. Like what? Pointing to the information desk!"

She was on the verge of tears again. Jim looked at her without moving. His sympathy had been completely eroded by the daily onslaught of similar complaints. Her helplessness had even begun to make him angry. "I think you should do what you've been talking about. Start looking for another job."

"God I can't do this anymore. I don't want to leave the kids though. And where else am I going to get a job?"

"Anywhere. A school. Columbus. There're plenty of places around. And they all have kids."

"Shut up."

". . ."

". . ."

". . ."

"OK I didn't mean that."

"Fine."

"..."

"..."

"Oh don't get angry."

"I don't want to fight about this. Just do something and stop complaining all the time. Quit or deal with her."

"Just because you don't give a damn about your job."

"I do a fine—"

"You don't give a fuck about your kids. It's easy to go to work every day when there's nothing you want. Just getting by like you always do."

"Alright. I'm not going to have this conversation. You're right . . . I don't think about the job the same way you do. You want a better job. Then get a better job. Either that or get Camilla fired. Make a complaint. Or quit. Or both. I don't know, I don't know how this became so important to you, but I can't really take all this complaining anymore."

"..."

"..."

"..."

"No. I can take it. It's not that. Just. Forget about it. Let's talk about it later."

"Fuck you, Jim."

"Fine."

"Fine."

◉ ◉

HE WAS DRIVING THIS TIME. Enough unusual that she could believe it wouldn't have happened if it had been her. Not that she would ever say such a thing.

At an intersection, the other car had turned in front of them too quickly for them to stop—though, to Judy, it seemed like they should have been able to.

Jim heard first a THUNK! then was thrown against his seatbelt slightly harder than he expected. They got out to find that everyone was OK. The other car had a small dent, but Jim and Judy's front end had collapsed.

The driver of the other car, a young woman, said, "I'm sorry."

"Are you OK?"

"I'm fine."

"Well let's call the police."

"Um, right. I live over there," she gestured to an apartment complex. "The thing is, I have to get to the airport."

"We have to call the police," Judy said.

"Yes. I know. Um. Yeah. Follow me."

Judy said to Jim, "You go. I'll wait here."

Jim walked beside the young woman as she led him to her apartment. Since he thought they could be legal enemies and since he knew nothing about the law, he was thinking very hard of any assumptions he could make about her.

She was in her early twenties. She was wearing a plain yellow blouse and a bracelet of large amber beads. Jim had noted that she'd had a sticker on her car with rainbow-shiny dancing bears. He'd always thought those were a Grateful Dead symbol but now wasn't sure. She could be a history undergraduate or a real estate office manager; really, he'd no idea. Was she a hippie of some kind? How did hippies handle fender benders?

She lived in a townhouse-style condominium in a complex of similar apartments. They had walked farther from the scene than he'd expected—but not that far really. Upon entering the woman's apartment Jim smelled potpourri.

From the kitchen, she called the police. Jim asked if he could call their insurance company. She left the room and went down the hallway, which Jim recognized as tactful, but wondered if they weren't acting unnecessarily wary of each other. When he was done, he asked her if she wanted to call her insurance company as well.

"I probably should huh. OK, you can wait in the living room."

Jim blinked then walked out of the kitchen.

Her living room oddly enough gave him no more information about her. He could tell only that she probably wasn't in college and that she didn't read much and had some interest in yoga.

But despite the generic layout, he was glad to have seen it. He wasn't sure if people, coming to *their* living room, would necessarily find any more interesting or informing details. It was simply a wonder to see, no matter how predictable, how others lived. The yoga video, the Madonna CDs, the venetian blinds. In the corner he noted a fantastic coat rack of dark wood, elegantly bare but for one red scarf and a leather jacket. He felt grateful that the accident had allowed him to see these things.

Judy stood waiting at the side of the road. She was too nervous to sit in the car with its front crumpled like that. Visions from the movies of exploding cars. It was cold though and she wondered what was taking them so long. She thought about their insurance rate and the cost of repair and how she was going to get to work. Strictly an inconvenience, she warned herself, and nothing to get furious about. The cop arrived at the same time that Jim and the other driver came back. The cop took the other driver's statement first and then came over to them.

"You were driving, right?" he asked Jim.

"Yes, officer."

"Am I free to go now?" the young woman asked.

"Yes."

After the questions, the cop gave them the report number and said, "You're lucky. She admitted right away that it was her fault."

Though it worried Judy to do so, they drove the car to a mechanic. The whole day was eaten up with waiting and phone calls and negotiating. Eventually Bill came to pick them up from the garage.

◉

DEAR MS. AUTOMOBILE—

Breaker breaker. Krshh. Do ya read me? Breaker breaker. Krssh. Where are you dear erstwhile wife. This is your long-lost husband calling. Breaker breaker. I'm in love with another woman now. Do you read me? Krsh. Skittle krsh. I'm in the middle of America now, planning my slow-cooked revenge by doing everything right, by doing nothing at all. Breaker breaker. Can you read me?

I'm in the middle of America, selling old stories, one of which is probably ours, though it would be hard for me to remember which. Maybe you could tell, but you'd have to go through the index and cross-check and even then I'm not sure you would. I've been thinking of love and what it means for men and women. Breaker breaker.

I also imagine that I'm talking through a CB like a trucker. Breaker breaker. Krsh. Krsh.

Dear Ms. Automobile, I've been trying to write to you for a long time now, though I don't know what I have to say. I figure you should get a progress report on the travels, though who knows if I'd want one from you. Do you remember when we used to have sex? When we used to fuck regularly? Do you remember any specific times, like glass glinting off the road you catch in your rearview as you drive your great big truck over a black ribbon through a white-salted desert? Over a table or on a couch?

I've bought a house with a woman. She's a librarian and exceptionally pretty to be with a man like me. She likes my intelligence and my defeat. I like her past victories and her survival skills. We're a good match. I make dinner some days and some days she makes dinner. We go to our jobs and pinch ourselves every day so we won't go numb from the pain that is seeing every day end without coming any closer to the promise that we saw once very clearly when we were younger. We wake up hopeful and go to bed stoic. We want everything from each other except fame and money, which would therefore mean we were doomed, except we won't be able to keep pinching ourselves and eventually will go numb despite the holding of breath and the hard blinking. Despite the knuckles grinding into our thighs and the cold water on our faces and the tongue biting, we'll fall asleep together in the bed we bought in our house we bought which we painted blue.

You? I think you're in some faraway place now working on an adventure movie. You're a film director now and are in charge of a cast of characters you wield like a weapon to draw blood and hunger from your audience of one. You're working on this adventure movie in some place where they speak a language that your mouth can't form the sounds of, and you're battling the script girl and the producer to get it done your way, which you don't really give a damn about except you know it's the perfect way so can't really give up despite not giving a damn.

Actually you're done shooting and now you're editing this movie that you've made. You've sent the whole crew home but are staying on, living and working out of a basement apartment in Latvia or Tijuana or Kuala Lumpur. Every day you're snipping and rearranging pieces of film so that there's a shimmer of knife-edge flowing from title shot to closing credits. You spend the whole day in a darkened room staring at the pulsating heart light of a flatbed projector. Your only company is a mute boy of sixteen years who hangs the smelly film onto a wall of hooks behind you. He doesn't label or organize but if you describe the scene you want he can take it down from one of the hundreds of hooks by memory. It is a painfully slow process but you can't seem to teach him any other way, and it's still quicker than if you did it yourself. He naps, curled around a stool, at your feet. I'm close, right? Admit it. I'm dead-on.

God, I envy you. I can say that now because I know you can't use it at all. It does you no good, doesn't even give you a lick of satisfaction. You never cared enough about me in the first place and you've almost forgotten my name by now. OK. Sorry. I know you remember me, and I know you cared for me. Maybe tomorrow evening I'll get drunk before I finish this letter . . .

Now the next day and it's funny. The dawn came and everything was washed away. I went to work and the sun came through the windows of the school building (I'm a schoolteacher now) and I lived a normal day. My bride-to-be (I'm getting married again) and I had dinner at a restaurant and talked about children and a honeymoon in Europe. Maybe we'll stop in Latvia and tour the old parts of the old cities. After dinner she went to bed, and I took down a bottle of scotch and came here to finish this letter. Here's my advice. In the last scene of the movie, your heroine, who's survived the pirates and the mafia and the bomb, should be cut down by an unidentified sniper. He'll just be a shadow in a window at the top of a tall building. Your heroine will be dressed to the nines at a champagne soiree where she's going to meet the man she almost lost but saved. A burst of blood will stream from her throat and splatter onto the white breast of her lover's tux. It'll be an absurd, left-field ending that will leave your audience of one transfixed because of how dully and easily it ties everything up. Just tack it on and stop handwringing about it. You know it's right. You shot the scene already. Just nudge the boy at your feet. Ask him. He knows which hook the film is on. Splice it in and call it a day.

Still there? Breaker breaker? Ksh. Ksh. This is all to tell you about the wedding, which will take place six months from now. September twelfth. Eight p.m. at the Hotel Chillicothe. We're registered at a few shops in town and at the Lazarus Department Store in Columbus. No RSVP necessary. Ksh. Breaker. You got a ten four? This is Nightflight Ranger looking for the Corvette Baby. There's a song on KLUV that I dedicated to you. DJ says he'll play it at midnight. It's our song, "Assassin of the Heart" by Johann Sebastian Bach. A hit when we were fourteen and the soundtrack to our lovemaking in our Chicago apartment. You were wet and I was erect. That's the way I remember it. And I love you very much. Judy is well and it's a lovely summer here in Ohio. The lake's drying up again and the kids are just dying to get out of the classroom and run around. We're busy with the wedding planning and I'm taking classes at night for my master's. Hope all is well with you. Best of luck.

Love,
Mr. Cloud

PART THREE MIRAGE

Frank

EASILY, SARAH ARRANGED to meet Frank for a drink. He was wearing storytelling clothes. Sarah thought he was a twist of a superhero, his business suit hiding his real costume underneath—another business suit. Frank rolled up his shirtsleeves, his forearms handsome and accustomed to subtle and conquering gestures. He pinched an atom of air in front of him above the table and shook it, guiding it through the space-time of his story, releasing it at the end of a sentence when it was no longer needed.

She relaxed her shoulders and widened her eyes. She looked at both Frank's mouth and his pinching fingers. She sat passively back, as his audience, hunting him. He said,

I would like to answer your questions but, to be honest, it isn't easy and I'm not sure you would believe me.

OK, yes,

Alright. Okay.

alright . . .

OK, if you're sure. Well, it has to do with the day I quit smoking. Which was the same day I started to lose weight. But, no, I should start before that, if you're sure. If you're really sure you want to hear about all of that.

No, I don't smoke any longer, I'll get to that, but,

alright. If you say so.

About three years ago at the end of December, I was invited to a friend's house for a New Year's Eve party. I lived then in Philadelphia. My friend at the time lived here, but she, she had, a close friend at the time, and she, she had incredible parties. So I had planned

I can't even describe them. She had a habit, her only real talent I can tell you, but to be an artist at all, in any way, well you see, you make allowances. Incredible allowances if you believe in them. And I really did. But she held completely mind-blowing parties. I don't mean recreationally mind-blowing. I mean parties that stay with you, that yes

Right, exactly, that *haunt* you for years. Until you've reviewed them over and over, as best as memory allows, and when you think you're over it, that you've somehow digested it and ex*haust*ed it, you'll go to another one, because it's usually a long time in between events, as it should be.

Yes, there is that thought. A kind of distrust, a skepticism, of the prolific. I agree. But anyway, this woman was an artist of, in my book, the highest caliber.

And the next party, and I made sure I always went to them, would awaken every instinct, every memory you had of the past and your heart would for days shudder in its, in, in its profundity.

she was *not* prolific, in fact I used to beg her to have another one. Well, I wouldn't openly, but I'd drop explicit enough

No, not really any clearer than that. There wasn't a theme I could explain, there was her personal texture, finally, her *way* of doing it, but other than that, and that is indefinable and unsayable, of course, and other than that, they were just parties.

Some big, some small. One was a dinner party with five of us, another a fuller gathering in someone's house, a house in the middle of nowhere.

Always some incredible people, but the right mix. Nothing so you felt the thing was too big for you, but somehow included you, that you too were important even as you stood next to Isabelle Huppert or Daffy Duck, I'm just making up names, but because celebrities came too; in fact, this was the only place I've ever seen a living-breathing *star.* The only place I've surely ever talked to one. But at the time, it was something you just accepted. I, I shouldn't've mentioned the celebrities. That was completely unimportant. Don't get stuck on that, it really wasn't

no, it wasn't the breadth, that's not the point, it wasn't like some supreme, like some taste test of culture's. No it wasn't well, I'm not sure what the final point of it was. I guess it was a party, simply, I mean a gathering without purpose but some lucky ceremony against solitude. They were not always fun

no, no, there were definite boring parts. Some guest would hog your time. Sure that happened, it was alive to those possibilities. I mean she could've crafted a perfect *ride,* if that's what you wanted, but well, she balanced it. At least you trusted it much more because it was free to be boring and grating and have these uncomfortable imperfect joints. You trusted that it was real, that it was happening.

You don't have to buy it. I understand. Just accept that I buy it, that I believed and

She's from the same town Jim and I grew up in. It's funny, I don't think he knows her. Well, I contributed to it. I'll admit. It's something you don't broadcast widely, once you know about it.

No, no Jim didn't know about it. I didn't want to share this. I kept it from him, to be honest.

But anyway, around that December I had got an invite for a New Year's party.

No, just a phone call from her. Nothing printed. Another aspect of these parties was that they were very informal.

Which was really incredible, if you believe what I've just described. I mean they were also fantastically constrained. I mean fantastically *formal* in a structural sense, but—no mention of dress code or even a time. Just show up, sometime around the usual time, she'd say.

And of course—now you can see why, or at least you can see my enthusiasm on the matter—I immediately accepted. And cleared my calendar around those days too. And on the day before the day, meaning December thirtieth, I rented a car and drove up to New York.

It was really an incredible feeling because I realized I had an awesome amount of faith in Judy's talent. Not in Judy maybe, but in her talent. And it is *very* rare that you realize you are in the hands of a true *maestro.* That a new production comes out, and you can have complete faith that it will be excellent. Maybe not a masterpiece every time, but at least excellent. Very few humans guarantee that type of quality every time out. So that here I had an almost overwhelming feeling of anticipation, but without any fear of disappointment, so not completely overwhelming, you see. Let's call it just critically short of being overwhelmed. Maximum whelmed, you could say. I'll tell you the drive up was incredible with this feeling.

Yes, I'm getting to that. All this is about that, really.

Yes, but let's get another. No, I'll get them. Please. Really. Same?

So this feeling of maximum whelming anticipation was unusual, for the time. And I drove up.

I was a little early. I had some time to kill. So I sat in my hotel room waiting. I'd watched an hour of television, but I was too restless for it to really zonk me out. So I decided to wander around the hotel some. And I got up off the bed and walked out of my room

and felt that double feeling of separation and belonging that comes with exiting your hotel room—do you know what I mean? That peaceful crushed-carpet change between your cell and the netherland between cells.

I was in the hallway.

And I remember thinking, This is an odd hotel, neither run-down nor well kept, but it is, cavernous. And not too well lit, either. But clean. Judy booked it for me. At the time, I'd thought, How thoughtful.

And I went down one hall and then another, just wandering around, and, after a while, was getting bored and ready to go back to my room, when I thought about the elevator.

I thought I'd go up to the top and have a look at the skyline, if I could see it.

So I found the elevator, and picked the largest digit I saw,

and went up.

And when the doors opened, there was a large gallery, a big room with large windows on all sides and big nicely smelling couches all along the walls

well, I smelled them. I smelled the odor in the room as soon as I walked in, and, no one else was there, which was a little odd, but not terribly because this lounge, or gallery, or whatnot, hadn't been advertised anywhere that I'd seen, so I didn't find it unusual that no one was there, but and so, I smelled a heavy flowery smell and when I had gone over and sat on the couch, I smelled it even more strongly so I casually bent over and sniffed it, and

the couches smelled. And beside the couches and on the small tables in front of the couches were ashtrays with no ashes in them. Very clean and asking to be defiled, so

I took out a cigarette and started to smoke it. Finally starting to enjoy myself—and relax. And it was a nice view, I could see Jersey, I guess it was, over the water and a big red crane doing some slow construction, which I'd watched for a while

and I decided I should enjoy the feeling of anticipation I was having about Judy's party, not work myself up about it, but just enjoy it and appreciate the sweet hum of my mind running toward the party in time. So I did that, just sat back and smoked and relaxed.

And as I sat there, I heard the elevator coming up, gently, and I was hoping that it wasn't going to unload anybody here, on my floor, right when I was beginning to relax but then there was a very loud, DING!

and I half turned toward the elevator, because I was sitting in a place where I had to crane a bit to see the doors, and I turned and the doors opened, but nobody came out.

The room wasn't lit. I mean there were lights but none of them were on, and the only light was from the windows and I think that contributed some. The feeling of privacy and some theft, some creeping onto a place where you're not supposed—because who doesn't turn on lights for a guest, save for intruder or intimate. And the doors just opened, and I and the lit-inside of the elevator—and at that moment it was the only artificial light in the room—and I and it just looked at each other, my two eyes to its cyclops, and after a few seconds, it winked closed and went back down.

And I was relieved. Greatly relieved I don't know why. I think I was very wound up, still, no matter I was telling myself to relax.

So I turned back toward the window and lit another cigarette, and put my head back on the couch and breathed deeply, trying again to relax, take in the heavy flower smell under my cigarette, look out the window, and relax

but I heard the elevator again. And this time I didn't turn my head, just listened. And again the whir of well-tuned machinery drawing near and again the, DING!

and I didn't turn around but the light in the room grew a bit. A small bit of directed yellow opened and closed a path through the fogged whiteness. And as the elevator hummed back down, as the sound of it grew more and more removed, another sound, a rhythmic sound, replaced it. One of steps.

Subdued steps, the sound of hard dress shoes on a medium-woofed carpet, is what I heard, coming toward me. And I didn't turn around, but the man, for it turned out to be a man, came into view and sat down across from me. He was wearing a dark suit and had his legs crossed.

He nodded and I nodded back, a minimum of courtesy but we did not go without the minimum, this man and I, I've often thought. He turned to look out the window and I did the same, turned my head a bit and looked out. And, after a while, I heard, but did not see, maybe I felt, I felt him turn back and look at me, take me in. Which I let him do, because there is the curiosity you accept from anyone and hope others accept from you

in a public place with spontaneous gathering. But he held it too long. He did not glance he looked hard up and down, I felt.

And as I was looking out the window, feeling myself looked at, I heard the whir again of the elevator approaching. I had begun to recognize the pattern, somehow, you may say it's illogical, but I had begun to know when the elevator was coming to this floor. Perhaps the floors directly beneath us were seldom used, and there was a statistical point that I had recognized, somehow, in two trials, that when passed, told me the elevator was coming.

But I heard it, at the moment, I heard the elevator come, and I knew it was coming to this floor. And I turned back toward the man and I was correct. He *was* looking right at me. The silence between us was being taken up by the elevator sound, not a loud sound, but the silence was quite silent, and he said,

"Do you want to trade souls?"

And I was in the elevator. DING! in the elevator, and

close doors, close doors, close doors.

New York City, I thought. Freaks everywhere. And I tell you, that elevator couldn't go down fast enough. It gave me the willies. I would say I didn't hear him clearly, that it was nerves, but I can put on the tape and rewind and hear the drawl of his voice, for he had one, a drawl, smooth and melodic, and I could hear that drawl and his question, absolutely crystal in my hearing's memory.

So I went back down to my room, and I sat for a moment on the bed. But it was too quiet, and even when I turned the television on, I was still feeling a little creepy, no matter the sound, so I decided to go for a drive.

Traffic was easy actually, and I drove, just driving with the heater on, not on full but a gentle heat circling around my toes, and every once in a while I would crack the window and have a cigarette, and then there'd be that terrific division of air, the numbing cold whip of wind on my left-hand side and the soporific cuddly warmth around my midriff, and after a while, after a real while because I was just going now, not thinking but going, and after a while, the land flattened or the buildings shrunk to normal and dispersed, and there were trees, see-through-able but netting the land. A real winter scene, save for the snow.

And I was very much enjoying it, the meditation, the blank mind of it, of driving. The anxiety of the hotel was fading, and I was starting to feel good, almost like the drive up had felt. My mind was empty of consequence save for what I chose to place there, and I chose only the distant pleasurable anticipation of the party.

Often, when there's something good coming up, I'll be unable to enjoy the time waiting, leading up to it. I'll worry about disappointment, that it won't be good enough, and I'll also worry about, well I guess similar to disappointment, that it's too precious, that even if it's good, it is—no matter the event because it is just an event, a plan—and it is such a delicate thing to hang so much good feeling upon . . . the measurement of its goodness is inversely proportional to this feeling of vulnerability, you see

but these things were kept distant. Were out of mind.

So that was the battle too, all this running around before, to not spoil it.

Other times I had tried to, or in other events perhaps, I'd try to keep my life normalized up till the last moment. Go to work or do the laundry or do whatever else I normally do, and break from the routine just at the last moment, to, like, trick the mind into thinking it wasn't really going.

But that never worked. The normal always let my mind go the furthest, always the immediate physical world was navigable without thinking, so that thinking would head elsewhere, deep into its own self-contained jungle.

So I knew that didn't work for me.

So this time, I'd rigged the time beforehand.

Work, at that time, was actually quite busy, no matter that I just said it was all somewhat mindless work. But the wrong kind of busy, I think, is the point. So but, I only got those couple days off.

And used them to drive to New York and position myself in unfamiliars to occupy my mind.

And it seemed to work.

So that now I was really, finally, truly, beginning to relax. I had a cigarette in my left hand, and the hand was cold to the touch for the window breeze, and my feet were toasty, and the air seemed devoid of particulate, clear to breathe and a little sweet.

But I knew I should get off the highway, otherwise I'd drive too far, so I turned off and began touring back roads. Backwaters and villages and small towns.

Through places not too different from where Jim and I grew up, in fact. Well, everything was different of course, but there was a distance between houses, between dwellings, the random sight of a little prosperity, a nice house for instance, ugly maybe, like an A-frame house, but with good wood and perfect ninety-degree windows cut into it, and a good car in front of it. And then a few miles down, an aluminum-sided house, faded yellow, plopped down in an expanse of land, nothing right-angled at all, the foundation, even, sloping into the ground, with half a city block between it and its wobbly mailbox with its chipped red flag permanently rusted to its side.

These things were the same. And it reminded me of that place, that so-called hometown. Which I never think of, but I never leave the city, so perhaps it's as simple as that. But I drove along some more, a tiny bit nostalgic, which really, I'm never.

Maybe, some people though *are* nostalgic for painful things. Though you're right in that sense, I'm not one of them.

But at that point I thought I'd had enough, or that it was as much distance from the city as I could afford, and decided to stop someplace for dinner and then drive back to the city.

So I saw a Friendly's and pulled in. I had, I remember, chicken-fried steak. And two cups of coffee. So I knew I should stop at the bathroom before I headed out, which I did.

And in the bathroom, as I was, forgive the picture of it, as I was in front of the urinal, I felt another glance, a familiar glance coming from the urinal next to me. So I looked left. Briefly, because this is not the same as a random public meeting, but a place of vulnerability, and I follow the etiquette, but to my surprise, there's the suited man again and he's again looking at me and says, again, "Do you want to trade souls?"

So I'm beyond baffled, beyond surprised. In shock I manage to zip up and take a step back and he does the same.

And in a clarity of shock, I ask, Where?

He points out and leads me out of the bathroom and out in the parking lot and

yes, well, right before he gets into the car, into the passenger's side of the car because he wants me to drive

yes, right before that, I think those thoughts, I think murder and rape and theft as immediate possibilities, but

but he had just appeared at two places miles apart, without direction, without, I'm pretty sure, vehicle, and I was just too impressed by his attention to me, and his ability to travel, to think to not follow it out.

Well, it wasn't bravery, it was shock and a giving up.

So he tells me the directions and I drive. I try starting a conversation with him but he doesn't answer, just points out directions. I then ask, Will it hurt, this trading of souls?

And he says, Not at all.

Are you sure, I ask. And he nods.

So believe it or not, after that, I'm relaxed. I trusted him. For, at that moment, I was only unsure if I could handle the pain of whatever traumatic or decisive event about to come. And once assured against pain, I was at ease.

And we drove on and on and the daylight was starting to wane and, finally, we came to a wood, and he directed us into the wood. And he said, There's a ceremony involved.

And I asked, completely relaxed, I must have been, to think this way at all, I asked: Is it necessary?

He actually seemed surprised at this question, and said, Well, yes.

Will it take long?

No.

So we drive through the woods and come to a clearing where a fire had been set up. A small campfire. And the man tells me to wait here and just *enjoy the show.*

So I turn the engine off and light a cigarette and just wait for whatever's to come.

That's what he said. Enjoy the show.

And he walked into the woods a little and came back holding what looked like a tin can with holes punched into it,

and then he bent over the fire, which wasn't huge but wasn't a small fire so that he had to shield his eyes a little bit and crouch down under the smoke to do this, and he quickly scooped up a bunch of hot rocks and burning twigs from the fire.

And then he set the can down and pulled out some string from his suit pocket and tied it to this tin can. And then he held the can from the string and started swinging it.

In dusky light, within a vertical plane, so the coals inside it began to define a bright yellow-blue circle, he whirled the tin can. And then he started jumping in and out of this circle of embers and whooped a few times.

I put down my cigarette and just watched him, concentrating on what he was doing—but that happened to be it. He put down the can and came back to the car.

It's done, he said.

That's it? I asked.

Yep, he said. And he picked up my cigarette which was burning in the car's ashtray, got out, and walked into the woods.

Sarah

I DESPERATELY WANTED OUT of the social contract. But I also didn't want to surrender everything and live only in my mind. How to get out of the contract, find a loophole, and yet not end up in the nation's waste bins: in prison, in a psychiatric ward, in Hollywood. That was the rebellion I wanted—to slip out, sane—what the teenage riot wanted to become before adulthood's insidious rationality plucked you from the singing barricades. That's why such an ambition must be puerile, because the idea always comes to one at thirteen.

At thirty-four, I had a plan. Not quite a complete vision, but a vision nonetheless. I had spent the year recovering from a divorce (marriage was a failed, aborted attempt at appeasement), trying to numb myself out by routine. But routine's numbness was only an anesthetic, while the bloody ministrations of surgery were taking place.

My plan was (is) to travel. Not travel, not to become a tourist, for that's its own nation with its own peripatetic constraints. (I had found that out the hard way, before my marriage.) Rather, I wanted (want) to find a place where the street signs are just glyphs not meant for me, and where the fear of the local confidence man is so strong I don't engage in the simplest of market conversations. New York City was close, you can be incredibly invisible here, but I needed that additional distance, the barrier of language and culture to tell me, finally, that I was outside it all.

I was almost there this summer. Only a few months of utter boredom and routine stood between me and a plane ticket to oblivion's next best thing. But old acquaintances surfaced, taunting me, saying I had unfinished business and I wasn't leaving until it was taken care of.

I balked and tried to walk away. But two men—two men's stories—(almost) stopped me from leaving. Only now, only today as I wait to board the plane, can I say with any confidence that my leave-taking will happen.

ABOUT A WEEK AFTER WE had had dinner, Frank disappeared. He was gone.

I went to his office. The entire office was gone. On the directory in the lobby, where his law office used to be, was now a magazine company.

I went back to my apartment, poured myself a drink, and did some thinking. So what? I told myself. What had really happened? Nothing.

Frank re-entered my life for a brief, mysterious instant and then vanished. So what. People did such things. And Mac? Well he was one of many lost souls, each, I'm sure, equally as tragic if not quite as bizarre.

I made up my mind then and there to resume life "as usual," to not think about the curious links that were chaining Frank, Mac, me, and Jim together.

I went back to my hack freelance work. No one had noticed I was gone. Not surprising. I'd been gone less than a month, not even a blip in the market's eternity. My savings, however, were not so untouched. I was broke. My friend Sonya's due date was only one month away and though I had planned on that birth date to coincide with my departure, now I'd have to extend my period of waiting by at least another six months.

I tried to bury myself in work. It's difficult but possible to shut off all thinking except those necessary to move the right papers around. Translate X. Fact-check Y. Proofread Z. Repeat till dead. The iteration was simple but required enough processing power to leave the rest of my head mercifully dormant.

For brief, troubling moments, I'd think to go find Mac, search the streets until I found him, if only to give him the news that I'd let him down, and to apologize.

Other times, I'd think of going to visit Madame Elster. This was the more disturbing thought because something told me this was supposed to be my next step. Frank, I'm sure, was somehow waiting for me there. He wasn't done with me, in fact, he might need me to go to Madame Elster's. It seemed, in my more dramatic dreamings, his life might even depend on my playing along. But, I thought, that was his mistake—not mine.

But it wasn't easy. Evading responsibility was exhausting. It took emotional energy to not care, but I was getting used to it.

When it felt like I was beginning to think too much, I went back to the old standbys. I saw a movie, let the lickability of the screen's candy-light sweeten my brain back to atrophy. Or I'd go swimming. It was a muscle routine, forth and back and back and forth. Elbow straight up out of the water, stretch, pull. It's amazing how few commands, forming a loop, could destroy time. Hours and then days and then weeks vanished like this.

Then Madame Elster called. The first two times I hung up on her. The third time, she pleaded, "Wait."

"I don't want to talk to you," I said.

"You were supposed to come by." This, by confirming my thinking, I now realized, was where I went wrong. I should have continued to hang up the phone, pulled out the whole box from the wall in a cinema-inspired act of violence. But then, maybe it was already too late. And rather I should have stopped before. Should have ignored Frank's thin profile that first afternoon, walking and back shadowed by summer light. Or I should have never married. Never traveled, never left home, never emerged from the womb.

It may seem I'm being fatalistic about my involvement, but there did seem a force, no matter what I imagined my options, which compelled me finally to enter mystery's heart. For that was what it was! Simply. No answers. Just ineffable mystery. A corpse, and signs as foreign and as meaningful to me as those incomprehensible street glyphs that I dearly wanted. (Want.)

No answers were forthcoming. But horrible, reality-rending, continuing mystery.

"According to whom?"

"It was your destiny . . ."

"You would know."

". . . And Mr. Exit prepaid for a session."

"He what?"

"He said you would come by and that I was supposed to give you a reading."

"No thanks."

"He's already paid for it."

"No, really. I'm fine without."

"He's also left a message for you."

"What is it?"

"I can't tell you unless you come in for a reading."

"He said this?"

"His instructions."

"OK . . . When?" And I re-entered.

Actually, it is the simpler mysteries that stay in the heart longest. The ones without any theater to them at all, just a prop and maybe a voice's inflection, but no murder or plot.

Today, before I left for the airport, I thought to take a walk through Central Park. One last good-bye to the city. I started in the park's northeast corner, in the Conservatory Garden. A violent, European raping and slaving of nature that becomes, if you let yourself forget, the sweetest, gentlest childhood memory.

I took a nap on a bench next to a walkway, shaded by a canopy of crabapple branches. A very still dream that didn't linger. When I awoke, my back was wet with sticky summer sweat.

I took a long walk down through the park. Coming to a small clearing that opened out of the wood like a room in a dream, I saw five Muslim girls playing football in their long black robes. Four girls chasing a fifth, all laughing, the football sometimes hidden in the arms of her dark, thick robe.

I walk into Madame Elster's office. A new secretary is there. Again: male. Dark features. An amazing and profound lust traps me again. I don't even want to make love to this man; he probably looks better in his incredibly tailored suit than out of it. But. I would give much to lie with him on an expensive and tasteful sofa, place my head on his chest, and pretend to be beautiful. Obviously Madame Elster is an outrageous pervert.

I follow him a too short distance to her office.

"Hello, why, you're drunk!" This is how she greets me. It is true, though rude. I'd been drinking since her phone call

(and, even now—provided for by the airport bar—have not stopped).

"Hello. Yes. And how can you hire such tasty men?" I could be frank too.

"It's all in the money, dearie, and after a while, they all lose their magic. Usually takes no more than a few weeks. Want some coffee?"

"How 'bout a drink?" I say, pushing, because I am supposedly the one doing the favor, by being here.

My instinct is right, because Madame—Ms.—Elster answers, "Why not?" and somehow, immediately, Mr. Olive-skinned-perfection arrives with two glasses of wine.

"What's Frank's message?" I ask.

"In due time," she says. "We have to do your reading."

"Fine, how's it done?" I ask.

She swivels in a chair to face a monitor sitting on her desk. "By computer," she says.

I gulp down my wine and pour freely from the bottle Olive-Skin has left on the desk.

"When and where were you born?" she asks. I tell her.

She tells me to cut a tarot deck. "Concentrate," she says. I do.

She looks at both my palms and asks me my blood type. I don't know my blood type. In a flash Olive-Skin has taken a sample of my blood. "We've an in-house lab," she explains.

It all takes fifteen minutes. At the end, she hits a button on her keyboard and I hear a printer's warm-up whir sounding from under her desk. She pulls out a page that she hands to me. She looks into my eyes and begins talking.

It takes a moment before I realize she is reciting word for word what's on the paper she's handed me. I keep looking down at the paper, back into her eyes, back down to the paper, back into her eyes. All along, her eyes are directed

straight into mine, unmoving, unflinching, radiating understanding and warmth. Her voice is gentle and beautifully singsongy. She says:

> Everything will go according to your plan. You will be a collector of mysteries. You will catch unfathomables, and keep them. Like a zoo. This is the only warning I will give you: By breathing and living in their emptiness, you will become nothing. This will not take away your hunger nor give you the gift of oblivion.
>
> In a week your friend will bear a child. All pregnancies are calendars. This birth will mark the end of your waiting and the beginning of your transition. This girl's name will be Hope, a plain, simple American name (though not very common), and you will bid it farewell.
>
> After your friend's birth, you will have some errands to run. Two of them are to find Frank Exit and the homeless man who calls himself Mac. When you find Mac, he will not care that you haven't delivered his message to Frank.
>
> Frank doesn't know anything about Mac. He gives Mac money every week only because I've told him to do so. Frank does this just on faith. It keeps Mac alive, even though his life is just a discarded shell. He was necessary for Frank's transformation. I advise you against telling Frank who Mac is because it is unnecessary, changes nothing, and would only make Frank feel guilty of something that he could not have avoided. Some, though not all, are unalterably shackled to Destiny. Such is the case with Frank and Mac. You do not have to believe me, but it is true. Mac will die in your presence.
>
> You will discover other people who work for me. This is not important but will show you that I can predict things, which might make it easier for you.

Though you never worried about this enough, you will not become an alcoholic. Yet you will stay drunk from now until your transition is complete. You will find the people who work for me enviably glamorous.

Though you will continue looking for him, Frank will be the one who finds you. He will offer you a choice. Unlike Frank Exit and Mac the bum, you are not shackled by Destiny. You have some choices to make, though admittedly your choices may only be costumed versions of one another.

This concludes the printout of your fortune telling.

I fold the paper four times and put it into my pocket. I refill my glass with wine. I am happy with the amount of detail in my fortune. I believe in it because it reflects my own intuition.

We may hope for our futures in such obvious ways that others, talented enough, can flatter us by articulating our own desires. Or maybe Madame Elster can see the future. Even if she turns out to be wrong, I am respectful of her insight.

"Thank you," I say.

"You're welcome . . . Would you like Frank's message now."

"Um, yes, please."

She hands me a fortune cookie.

I break it in two and eat half of the cookie while uncurling the strip of paper upon which is written Frank's message. It says, "I will help you write your suicide note."

I eat the other half of the cookie.

I will help you write your suicide note.

I went back to my apartment. I took out an almost empty bottle of scotch and put ice in a glass. I poured myself a drink and placed the curled-up fortune on my desk. Then

I stared at it for a while. I thought, calmly at first, I am not killing myself.

But it started to haunt me. Maybe I *was* thinking about killing myself. Maybe that was the foreign country I was destined to go to. The undiscovered country. But no. I am a practical woman. Suicide is not usually the option taken by practical people.

The "usually" that I have put into that sentence scares me.

Am I secretly (keeping it even from myself) planning on murdering myself?

LIKE CLOCKWORK . . . like clockwork, Sonya's baby was born one week later. The last day of the last month of my imaginary calendar had flown off. The words on the screen read: Time passes. I didn't want to ask, but Dan told me the baby's name: Hope. It was Dan's grandmother's name. I said goodbye to the whole family, ending with Hope.

The next day I hesitated. I thought about ignoring Madame Elster's printout. I could stay home, continue my life, keep distant from all the hocus-pocus in the world. But I knew that I really didn't have a choice. I had to go out looking for Mac.

I started outside Frank's office. It hadn't occurred to me that if Frank had disappeared, Mac would also be lost without his ghost patron. Now he had even less anchor in the world. He wasn't in front of the building. I looked everywhere, but already another coffee cup, held by another's hand, was jingling in Mac's place. As if the message had been sent out: Vacancy.

I went uptown to where Frank lived. The doorman wouldn't even tell me if Frank had gone on vacation. Mac was again nowhere to be found. I decided to get a drink.

In the same bar where I'd once drunk after following Frank and Ms. Elster, I wondered again if they were a couple. Was Elster less a psychic than another of Frank's pawns, encircling and trapping me? I loathed (loathe) this bar.

I got very drunk.

After leaving the bar, I wandered around town looking for Mac some more. It wasn't easy. He could be anywhere. Yet I had faith I'd find him. Elster had said as much, though not much could be said of my sleuthing praxis, which involved wandering from bar to bar, tending my drunkenness as if it were a hothouse flower.

At this rate, I wasn't going to make rent this month. I was drinking up my savings. Somehow it didn't worry me. I'd hit up Ms. Elster. Or Frank, if I ever found him. When I stepped out of the bar, it was somehow noon.

I decided to eat. I went and got myself a plain bagel and a Budweiser and sat in Bryant Park.

Something told me Mac was nearby. Maybe next door . . . I went into the Rose Reading Room at the library. Rows of tables crowded with diligent readers. I took a seat at the edge of the large room and looked across. My eye took a snapshot. It was titled *The Beautiful Fiction of Democracy.* It won prizes in both photojournalism and conceptual art.

I closed my eyes and looked through the photo for Mac. In my binge, I realized I was becoming a less practical woman. In fact, knowing (for I had faith in Elster) my future, I no longer cared. This allowed a freedom, a loosening of my previous obsession with binaries and order. Mac was in my photo. He was in a row across the room, still in the T-shirt and neon-orange sweat pants I had bought him. He was hunched over, reading. I took the photo into my darkroom and enlarged it. Viewing the print through a magnifying lens, I saw he was reading a book on karma and the transmigration of souls.

I opened my eyes. Mac was just getting up. He pushed his seat back and left the desk, leaving his book. I surprised my neighbors by reacting violently, scratching, I'm sure, the tiled floor as I thrust my chair back and ran across the room. I paused next to Mac's seat long enough to check the title of his book. It wasn't a book on karma, it was Rimbaud's *Illuminations.*

He moved fast, or I moved slowly. I lost him. Though I realized that if I concentrated, I could feel if he was close by or not. It was like a childhood game of Hot or Cold. I closed my eyes. He wasn't that far away. I followed him into the subway and ended up in Brooklyn. Each time the subway stopped I closed my eyes and checked to see if he was still on the train. Hot? Cold? He got out at Sheepshead Bay. I entered a bar. I must have just missed him, or he was in the bathroom. I could feel that he was very close. I ordered a drink and tried to watch the bathroom door. No one came in or out. As I finished my drink, I heard the wind from the street as someone left the bar. Turning my head, I realized Mac had tricked me. He must have been hiding behind me the entire time, waiting for the right moment to flee. He chose the exact moment when my eyes were distracted, watching the last drops of scotch fall from the glass into my throat. I ran out into the street, but I'd lost him. I went back home to rest up. Chasing Mac wasn't easy.

The next day was hot. I made myself a martini. I went to the bathroom and looked in the mirror. I pulled down my lower lip and looked at my veiny gums. Drunk!

That evening, I followed Mac's scent into a Malaysian restaurant on the corner of a bustling block somewhere between

Chinatown and Little Italy. As soon as I entered, I knew Mac was inside—somewhere.

I told the server I was waiting for a friend and took a seat at the bar. I ordered a coffee and, when no one was looking, poured into it a healthy dose of whiskey. (I'd come prepared.)

There was a mirror behind the bar, which was convenient. Mac wouldn't be able to sneak past me so easily this time. Reflected in the mirror I could see my neighbors at the bar. There were three of them. I couldn't tell what they looked like because, strangely, they were all holding up books so that I couldn't see their faces. The first was reading what looked like a comic book called *The Tao Speaks* by Tsai Chih Chung, the second was reading something called *Bob and Alice's 1001 Best Jokes,* and the third was reading *The Auto Repair Manual for Meteorologists* by Winchell Factor. I knew one of them was Mac and it was just a game of figuring out which.

Immediately, as if they could read my thoughts, all three of them suddenly got up and left the restaurant.

I threw some money on the counter and followed them out the door. When I came out, I could see they had all gone down separate streets. I had to choose one to follow. I picked the guy with the joke book. I followed him for several blocks and saw him enter a movie theater. I bought a ticket and followed. A Hitchcock film was playing: *Vertigo.* It was one of my favorites. The film had already begun when I walked into the theater, though it was still near the beginning. I got sucked into the film as Bob-and-Alice knew I would. It was meant to be a distraction. Half an hour after I'd walked in, I suddenly remembered why and looked around. Bob-and-Alice was gone. My face burned with embarrassment at having been thrown off so easily. I left the movie theater and walked aimlessly until dawn and then went to my apartment for a few hours' sleep.

When I woke up the next day, I left my apartment and went to Tompkins Square Park and stared up at the building Mac had claimed was a brothel. Vodka and heat triggered a sudden lust. The summer and sex and the city. What a consonance! I saw the asphalt ooze with jism and pussyjuice and sweat.

I buzzed the door and prepared to make up a lie, but the door rattled with its electric pulse and I went inside. I wondered how such a place could be so lax in its screening of visitors. As the elevator opened, I saw a desk to my left, and behind it, to my surprise, was a man I had seen somewhere before. He looked up and said, "You're Sarah. Am I right?"

He was Elster's secretary, not Olive-Skin, but the first one, Action-Hero. "Yes."

I took a guess: "Could I have a drink?"

"Certainly."

"I'll have a scotch." He left and came back with a glass of red wine. I sighed and accepted it. After I'd taken a sip, he said, "The boss is waiting for you."

This was gratifying to my ego. Maybe all rooms and all doors had someone waiting for me.

Action-Hero led the way, down a hallway, to an office. I noticed he'd corrected the imperfect crease in his pants and gotten rid of his freckle. He led me to an office.

"Hello, you're drunk!" It was Madame Elster.

"Yes, and how do you get such tasty men." Evidently Madame Elster was a *Madame* Madame also.

"It's all in the money, dearie. Two weeks, tops, before you find the need to move on. By the way, Frank paid for a session for you here too."

"I was supposed to come here."

"Obviously."

"I don't want one. Really."

"How 'bout a foot massage."

"Hmm, um, OK."

I had a choice. Seven men were brought out. Action-Hero was among them, though disappointingly, Olive-Skin was not. They were individually striking, though as a group, I was overwhelmed by the number. It was a question of the whole being much less than the sum of its parts. My lust dried up. Madame Elster suggested a dark-haired boy who looked nineteen. She said he only spoke Serbo-Croatian and Japanese, that his name was Hiro and he was the best when it came to feet. He took me into a sparsely though tastefully furnished room and took off my shoes.

While he was giving me my foot massage I nodded off. I dreamt that I was wandering through the brothel. It had many rooms, all empty. In the last room I went to, I found Madame Elster making love to Olive-Skin. I said, "I envy your taste and easily spirited hedonism."

"I knew you would," she said over Olive-Skin's shoulder.

After my foot massage was done, Hiro and I had sex. Sometimes it felt like—though this was obviously untrue—I was deflowering him. Other times his foreign, blue pillow talk revealed a pastime of many elegant perversions.

It was metaphorically intoxicating, but when we were done, I wanted a drink. I asked for a scotch. He brought me a bourbon. Progress.

I MUST HAVE BLACKED OUT. I woke up in a clear white light. Someone's bedroom. There were two doors. One was ajar and looked like it led to a bathroom. The other was closed; I assumed it led to the rest of the apartment. On a chair were my clothes. I quickly washed my face and dressed. I remembered Mac's taunt: "It is an incredible feeling to wake up and not know why you are in a wood, to not know that it is actually dusk and not dawn, to not know your own name. Try it sometime." I checked myself. I didn't know where I was, or the time, but I did know who I was. This was immensely comforting.

I smelled coffee brewing and went out the door into a living room. I was in a spacious penthouse apartment. I went to the kitchen and poured myself a cup of coffee. Looking around greedily, I found a liquor cabinet and poured Irish whiskey into it. Through a window I could see a rooftop garden. Someone was there, pacing, maybe waiting for me.

It is a thrill to constantly walk through doors and have people waiting for you. The city then becomes a game board. I began to think Exit's manipulations were actually benign, perhaps even friendly.

I pulled open the sliding-glass door and walked out to the garden. The roof was sun bleached and the plants were green and thriving. My host continued pacing. He was a skinny man, wearing a white linen suit, complete with matching white shoes and tie. Otherwise his features were dark. He was tanned with dignified streaks of gray in his otherwise black hair. His goatee also had flecks of gray in it.

I said, "Good morning." He stopped pacing as if he'd just noticed I'd come out. He smiled and said, "Morning. I've been waiting for you," revealing a comforting Southern twang. He looked toward the horizon, or maybe the building's edge. He suddenly burst into a sprint and jumped off the edge.

I glanced toward the horizon. I wanted to laugh. How funny it was to wake up in a white room, make yourself coffee, and watch a man blithely kill himself. I placed the coffee cup down on the concrete roof and walked over to the edge.

I saw his body, outlined in the vertical distance. A crowd was gathering. This seemed wrong to me.

I decided to go down and look. I left the apartment.

I felt a panic welling up inside my chest. I told myself to take deep breaths. The elevator ride down was slow, claustrophobic, and anxious.

Coming out into the street, everything seemed as it once was, and I suddenly realized that there were probably very few rooms left with people waiting for me inside. A crowd had gathered as well as the police, and I could hear an ambulance coming. In the center of the crowd was the body. Some people averted their gaze, while others looked on, wide-eyed.

I looked.

The body was not dressed in a white suit and was not skinny. In fact, it was Mac the bum and he was still fat, though now sadly crooked and sickeningly, truly, broken. He was wearing a black suit.

I walked away.

On the way back to my apartment, I managed to buy a bottle of scotch. I sat in my apartment and drank. Suddenly I had a thought.

I looked for the trash bag that held Mac's suit. With great relief, I saw it was in the corner, where I had last left it. I went over and opened it up. The suit was there but it looked different, shrunken. And it was somehow now folded and clean. I put it on and sat for a while longer, drinking my scotch.

THE AIRPORT BAR IS OVERPRICED. I'm drinking vodka as a kind of tribute to my destination. I've held off thinking about these events as long as I could. As they were happening I tried to accept them, to not panic or even judge. In some ways, it is very simple. An everyday ambition: I want (wanted) to leave my life. I'm fed up with compromises and constraints and I'm, fortunately or not, unattached. So I can. The preparations were straightforward. But then Frank steps into my life again and makes everything zig and zag. It's no longer straightforward. I won't lie: it was exciting to be surprised and expected. For rooms to wait for you. And I, for a moment, believed that the mystery could continue, unfading and always. The fact is, however, for all that happened, nothing changed. I just go straight onward and this zigging and zagging summer I'll remember as only a zero-sum zenith.

Frank

AFTER SARAH LEFT, I moved into her apartment.

Madeleine Elster told me to do it, and I more or less do everything Madeleine tells me to do. At first I didn't see Madeleine's point and was annoyed. Sarah had left in a hurry, just packed a bag and left, and the apartment was still cluttered with her things. Since it was much smaller than the place I'd been living before, I didn't bring most of my stuff. Just a few suits to go to work in. In total it was only a small greasy kitchen and a shabby room furnished with only an equally shabby couch (too large for the room) and a generic desk alongside a lumpy bed. I had faith in Madeleine's talent though and, after a while, I got used to it.

More. After a while, I came to see it as something else. I slowly realized that I'd stumbled onto something. Well, not stumbled, more like directed to it. But I began to realize, after a few weeks, since I refused to really "move in" as it were, I realized that the apartment was an incredible recording of Sarah. It was as if I'd found an outrageously personal diary. A document of her life that she wasn't even aware of having written. So Madeleine again turned out to be right. I spent my days, which had been getting somehow lonelier, somehow emptier, a little bit at a time . . . well, I now spent my time reading over the inexhaustible book of Sarah.

Sarah's book I guess, more than others, could only be written this way. The eventlessness of her life, the silent inarticulable poems, could only be found in the dark strands left in her hairbrush. In the haphazard yet systematic ordering of her bookshelves. In the sculpture of pots left to dry in her dish rack.

I read her eagerly, every night, absorbed in the chapters of her toothbrush, of her answering machine message. One night I would gallop and sweat to the adventures of her pen jar—her work! after all. And on another night, I would read the sad eroticism of her very practical underwear drawer, of her medicine cabinet—and that night, I fell asleep masturbating to the rhythm of a (too easily recognized) lonely and antiseptic sex life. Her bathroom sink held encyclopedia volumes. Her sock drawer was a novel. Her dust motes, songs. I flattered myself to think that I knew her.

I studied these all and, furthermore, was careful after my initial realization, to disturb as little as possible. I kept intact everything: the smallest patterns of her carpet, the exact arrangement of her desk papers. I left her dirty laundry in the hamper and ate out so as to not deplete her spices by one flake or grain. But still, after months of this, I realized, sadly, that time and my presence were having their effect. No matter my archival intentions, the book that I was reading avidly every night, the book that, in a very real way, was saving my life—that book was slowly being erased, was crumbling to dust, disintegrating, even as I read it.

Just a few months after I'd moved in, the book was gone. The laundry was still left, soiled in the hamper, her shampoo bottles were still precisely that empty, but somehow her story was gone. I was there now, filling up the space, overcoming it with my smells and habits. It was now my apartment. Sighing, I told Madeleine this at our next session, thinking she'd be pleased that her lesson had been learned. I thought I could now move back to my own place, and keep the memory of having read Sarah's book. I thought it would be the next level of Madeleine's lesson, to then watch the secondary disintegration as those details themselves would lose edges in my remembering.

But Madeleine told me to stay on. I doubted her judgment. What more was there to learn? But the doubt was weak and my faith in her talent won out. And I stayed on.

I decided that keeping the apartment intact was no longer possible and, rather than delude myself and rather than corrupt the memory of the book any more than was necessary, I made it my own. I ceremoniously washed her laundry, packed the pots that had been drying in that dish rack for over a year. I kept what I thought I could use and moved the rest into storage. I bought a smaller couch, a more comfortable bed. I lined the shelves with my own books. One night, near the end of this transformation, I crouched over the small black machine on her bedside table and said, "Hello, you've reached Frank Exit. I'm not at home right now, but please leave a message after the tone."

THE YEARS RIGHT AFTER my weight loss I'd been thankfully at peace with a host of tormenting demons, led by a triumvirate named Loneliness, Jealousy, and Need. As soon as I met Sarah I could feel them inching closer again, ready to overtake me once more. But after she left, after Madeleine's advice to move into her apartment, I had somehow become strengthened, by reading Sarah's book, against these spirits. I was afraid that after the book was gone, my anxieties would return. But soon it became clear that I had been fortified, and that if they did come, I would be able to deal with them with some kind of melancholic but calm acceptance.

A few years went by. I met with Madeleine every week and wondered out loud occasionally if it was still necessary to live in that apartment. She just quietly told me it was, so I continued there and as well was living with a certain backbeat of anticipation. Maybe something else would happen to me after all, I thought.

Those years, when I droned steadily through my life, when my workweek was only interrupted with my visits to Madeleine and her brothel, were kept in sync and regular by that anticipation's low, murmuring pulse.

And then the invitation came.

It wasn't addressed to me, of course, which was a problem. It wasn't even from Judy. How strange it was, I thought, for Judy to have finally met Jim and now, even more strange, that they were going to get married. Still, what I was most struck by, what most excited me, was that Judy was going to have another party. A wedding.

The invitation wasn't from Judy, and the letter was an awkward calling out, by Jim, for redemption and judgment from his former wife. At least that's how I read it. But the fact that it was an invitation was clear, and—even if it was addressed to Sarah, I knew that I was going to attend in her place.

I wasn't always what might be called a mystical person. It came about because of my weight loss. My being born-again is another way, maybe, to say it. Before, I was more average. Crossed my fingers or knocked on wood to make a point in a conversation. But never really hesitated if I had to walk underneath a ladder. A broken mirror or a hat on a bed didn't send any shivers down my spine. Logic and reason and other machines of man. Those were my tools.

Now, they didn't get me very far, also, that must be said. Well, it's a simple person who's satisfied with only what they're taught in school. Gravity is a force. One plus one equals two. But everyone comes to understand, after a while, that the pull between bodies is unexplainable and profound. And one and one usually equals zero.

I'm not talking about symbolism. I'm talking about the uselessness of certain endeavors to do anything except maybe make your toast in the morning or give you a more seductive whiff of aftershave. Which, absolutely, I love a hot golden piece of toast in the morning, and I go weak in the knees myself upon smelling a new shade of cologne stepping past me. Who doesn't? But there came a time when those things mattered less to me. Very little. And a tall well-shouldered man didn't move me. Nor did the buttery aroma of the tastiest meal.

At that point in my life, in my thirties, I'd hit a certain wall. The one thing I can say for myself is that I didn't retreat when I hit it. I could have, and I imagine other people do, turn right back around and pretend they never saw the wall. Or drag their feet through life so as to never come to it at all. But I'd hit the wall and I kept banging my head against it until I was exhausted and frightened. Until I was defeated and numb.

Then I went to a party that changed my life.

At that party, Judy's first, I realized that there were greater possibilities than toast and aftershave or even broken mirrors and black cats. That there were paths of strange adventure and love open to me. I had known a sorceress. That's the only way I can explain it, but that's what she was.

She, herself, is not very impressive. Back then she was a dilettante-ish conceptual artist by night and graduate student by day. Now, she's about to get married and is living as a librarian in the Midwest. If you met her, you'd expect—and get—polite meaningless conversation about the current war or the psychology of marriage.

Her parties though. They were . . . well I've described them to others with no success, but they were for me—and all guests and witnesses corroborate—they were stunning. Each and every one punctuated, like elegant and surprising question marks, the dull speech of our lives. And the last one that I went to truly did change my life.

BUT THIS WILL BE the only one that I've ever crashed. I've always been invited, but somehow, since the last one, I've lost touch with Judy. I've lost touch with a lot of the people from my past, but Judy was the one person I hadn't meant to lose. It was a shock then, after all this time, to intercept the letter and find her marrying Jim! But after my years training with Madeleine, I realized that coincidence was just my generation's name for magic, and that there is a discovery, repeated by each generation, that magic is less extraordinary than it is hidden, and that once discovered, it becomes everywhere apparent.

IT WAS TO BE A SEPTEMBER WEDDING, nearly six months away. I had that long to prepare. For some reason I hesitated telling Madeleine about it, even though I thought she might know. After all, she had encouraged me to stay in Sarah's old apartment, and it seemed obvious for this exact reason. But I hesitated and it turned out that I was right to do so.

Madeleine told me not to go.

She looked surprised, even, when I told her, then sighed and told me it wasn't my place. I nodded but I knew that this would be the one ordinance of hers that I would break, that my faith in another's talent was going to override my faith in hers. I'm sure she knew this. Maybe not at the time, but as the months passed and we neared the date, I'm sure she realized that I was going to disobey her. I give her credit for never bringing it up again.

I BOOKED A PLANE to Columbus and reserved a rental car. On the day of my flight there was a freak lightning storm in New York. I thought Madeleine might have even greater powers than I had assumed, but the storm passed. I had been delayed an entire day, though, and would arrive late to the party I was about to crash.

I arrived in Columbus at night. With the two-hour drive to town, I wouldn't arrive until after eleven. When I did make the town, though I had grown up there and knew roughly where it was, I was a little worried I'd have trouble finding the hotel.

It was an oddity, a huge old hotel located just outside of town. When I was growing up, it had been a dilapidated shell. All the windows had been broken; the garden had overgrown to take over the entire back. High school kids from town had used it as a hangout and it was always strewn with broken glass and trash.

I missed the turnoff once, and made a right when I should have made a left, but eventually got my bearings. Though I did doubt myself when I finally did see the hotel. For some reason, I was assuming I'd find the same wrecked building that had always been there. Driving through miles of black country night, it was a surprise then to come to it, at the bottom of a small valley, flooding the area around it with light. Every light in the building was on. The hotel had been reconstructed. All the broken windows had been fixed, the facade had been painted, the woodwork repaired or replaced. I was amazed and wondered if Judy had done all this for her wedding.

There were several cars on the front lawn, so I parked the rental beside them and then entered the hushed, well-lit vestibule.

No one was there. I rang the bell on the lobby desk and no one came. Wandering around I saw a flicker of light out a back window. Looking out I saw that everyone was in the back. The lawn, now trimmed and bordered by small shrubbery, was revealed to be much larger than it had seemed in my childhood, and I could also see that someone had cut back the garden so it now tamely occupied a browning, vined corner. About seventy people were there mingling comfortably, sipping drinks.

I walked around the building to the back. The lawn was being lit by several small bonfires and hanging paper lamps. It was a warm summer evening and everyone was dressed casually and talking in low voices. It seemed like nothing had really happened yet; people were looking around, still waiting, which I took to be a good sign. I was offered and took a glass of wine and tried to not attract too much attention.

A few moments later I saw Judy. She was dressed in a simple dark-green dress and looked the same as I remembered. Long brown hair, an aristocratic face, a dancer's lithe build. Just then I thought she saw me, but instead of coming over she walked up to a small elevated podium and began to speak to the crowd.

"Hello. Now that all the guests have arrived, we might as well begin. I'd like to thank you all for coming, for helping Jim and me celebrate our wedding. I thought maybe we could get to know each other by playing a little game. Most of you have picked up your cards from the table over by the porch. If you haven't, please come and take one, and you'll see your assignments. OK . . . Let's begin."

Games had always been the opening sequence in Judy's parties. They served as icebreakers and usually were outrageous enough, or at least unorthodox enough, that the guests would be forced to, if not get rid of, then at least question some of their party-attending habits. Some of us, people who had been to Judy's parties before—and I recognized a few faces—already knew to follow instructions and be prepared for anything. But even for us these games were still necessary for Judy's plan, in order to train and re-train our expectations.

So I was excited. I hadn't missed anything at all, had in fact arrived just in time for things to begin. I walked over and looked for Sarah's card. There wasn't one, but there remained one which read "Replacement Guest," so I guessed that Judy had prepared for me after all.

Positions along the lawn's perimeter had been marked out. We had all been assigned one of these as our starting point. I went to mine at the far end of the lawn near the garden. There I was given another card of instructions.

Opening it I read,

When the man in front of you bows, you should do one of the following three things:

1. Take off all your clothes or
2. put all your clothes back on or
3. scratch your head as if you are thinking hard about something.

You may choose either the first or third of these to begin, but will have several opportunities to do all three. Thank you.

I took my place in a line. Each group evidently had a path though the lawn, crisscrossing it several times and intertwining with other lines. After the man in front of me had gone ahead about seven paces, I was instructed to begin my path across the lawn.

At first I concentrated on what the man in front of me was doing. I was wondering if I would have enough time to take off all my clothes or put them back on in the time it took for him to take one bow. So I started by scratching my head. I shouldn't have worried. He took a full minute to bow and another full minute to bring himself upright.

Scratching my head, I could also see what everyone else was doing. A man drank slowly from a beer. A woman was pantomiming a horse. Still another was making a full-faced grin but not showing any of her teeth. There were other bowers and other head scratchers and across the lawn I saw someone else now completely naked. The man in front of me had finished his bow and we all began to walk forward another few steps.

Every seventh step brought new episodes to watch, as well as a concentrated effort to complete your own performance effectively. As we continued, my thoughts would go back and forth between absorbing what everyone else was doing and seeing how well I could put my clothes on or off, or how I could best act out "hard thinking."

We kept at it for some time. There was a little talking and some laughter, but for the most part we were all absorbed in the events around us. A few people begin singing. Different parts to different songs at different moments, but it soon began to take the form of a strange round. Sometimes two or three people would come together and hold hands or kiss or pantomime a violent act or pass something between them.

It was a powerful ritual, though for what or symbolizing what was difficult to say. About halfway through, we were exhilarated. It was a grand dance, a pagan rite, a fascist architecture of people's smallest actions. I lost track of time, maybe it lasted an hour. I tried to see it from above, the slow-paced ballet of seventy-odd wedding guests.

At the end Judy just once again got up on the podium and said a simple, "Thanks," smiling. We applauded our efforts and laughed. As an icebreaker it had worked wonderfully. Soon, we had refreshed our drinks and were talking actively about what had just happened, exchanging reflections and interpretations.

I found out that the man in front of me was an ex-Tibetan monk originally from Georgia, who had met Judy when they were both going to library school. A man who I had seen scratching his head with me turned out to be a music teacher at the school where Jim worked. His wife, who had sung beautifully and who had also done a good horse impression, was a local journalist.

In the midst of our mingling, Judy walked by. She said hello to all of us, called each of the others by name, except carefully avoided mentioning mine. Anyway, I was glad that I wasn't being called out as an uninvited guest.

I said to the man next to me, "So you've been to Judy's parties before?"

"Yes."

"Were you at the one in Chicago, at the top of that skyscraper?"

"On Halloween? Yes, who were you?"

"I, I was dressed as a, I was a trash bag. I wore a trash bag around myself."

"That was you! I remember now," and he burst out laughing. "That was the absolute worst costume!"

I laughed with him. "Yes, yes it was, it was more of a symbol than a costume."

"Oh," he said, laughing less.

"I'm Frank," I said.

"Jacob. You looked completely different then."

"Thank you."

At that moment, something I'd been dreading happened. Jacob spotted Jim walking toward us. He whispered to me, "That's the groom, right? I haven't met him yet."

And before I could stop him he waved Jim over. I was steeling myself for whatever fallout was about to come over my disappearing act. Jim was smiling but also looked a little lost. "Hi," he said.

"Hello, thanks for having us," Jacob started.

"Good, good. You're enjoying yourselves."

"Yes. Very much. We like your, we were just saying how much we always like Judy's parties."

"Good. Yes, I've heard some other people say the same. I had no idea, actually, she did this." Jacob and I didn't look at each other. "So you must be friends of Judy's."

"Yes I'm Jacob and this is—"

"My name's Axel. Axel Burberrysmith. Garcia."

"Um, good. . . . Nice to meet you both. I'm going to go get a drink, would you like one?"

"No, I think we're fine."

"Good, good. Nice to meet you," and he walked away.

When he was out of earshot, I turned to Jacob to explain but he just laughed.

"What*ever* Axel Burberrysmith. Garcia."

"Well, I wasn't really prepared—"

"And did you get that about him not knowing Judy gives parties? What's that about."

"Don't know," I said. I was still amazed Jim hadn't recognized me.

AFTER A LITTLE WHILE Judy's voice was projected over a loudspeaker. She must have been speaking from a distant corner because everyone was turned in that direction, though I couldn't see her.

She said, "Thank you all again for coming. On the cards you picked up before, if you turn them over, you'll see three room numbers printed on the back. Choose any of these numbers to begin with. When you get to a room, you will meet others with the same room number. Your job is to exchange with three people over the course of the night some possession of your own that will serve as a party favor. I'll let you all figure out what three items of your own you'd like to exchange. If no one appears in a room, try the others. I will leave the sleeping arrangements for you all to figure out on your own.

"The formal ceremony will take place tomorrow morning at nine thirty. I'll see you all then. Thanks and good night."

A hiss and then the PA went out. A twitter of childlike excitement rippled across the crowd. Evidently, for her wedding, Judy was going to have us play an adapted form of spin the bottle. Despite my faith in Judy, I was having doubts, though the crowd seemed to love it.

People soon began drifting in search of rooms and roommates for the night. Jacob turned to me before leaving and said, "Meet me out front at three unless—you meet someone. I'll do the same." I laughed and nodded and then he left. As the crowd started to empty, I reached into my pocket and read the three room numbers that were assigned to me. Around me were only a few couples who were negotiating their own somewhat more constrained plans. Gritting my teeth, thinking this party was going to end up being a lot of work, I went to my first room.

IT WAS ON THE FOURTH FLOOR, the top floor, I think, of the hotel. There was still a good deal of mingling on the first two floors and several people talking on the stairs, but when I got to the third floor there were fewer, and the fourth was entirely empty. The only sound was the distant chatter filtering softly up from below. My room's door was open. Jim Fog was inside.

"Oh hey—it's Axel, right?" he said. "Funny to get the people you've already met."

"Must be fate."

"Having fun."

"Oh yeah. Great time."

"Good. Good."

I was as surprised that he remembered my goofy alias as I was that he still didn't recognize me. I walked over and sat next to my childhood friend, put my elbows on my knees and assumed a position I thought real men would assume to signify repose.

For a moment I was awash with memories. Creek beds, shared beers, and picked-up checks. Then I remembered arguments, loneliness, and blame. Then smells and light and long-ago shedded skin. I stared at my shoelaces.

"What should we trade?" he said.

"What?"

"As a souvenir, what favors do you have?" He was smiling and trying to be friendly, to bridge the awkward situation—that much more awkward, it felt, for me.

"Um, I don't know. What do you have?"

"Well, I don't know. I've got, well I happen to have this blank piece of paper, a breath mint, what else do I have . . ." He began feeling his pockets.

I continued to stare down at the ground. He must have thought I was unbearably shy. I noticed his shoes were similar to mine. "I've got an idea," I said.

"What?"

"Let's exchange shoelaces."

He stopped patting his pockets and looked over at my shoes and smiled. "Hey that's not bad. They're almost the same. Just yours are a darker brown. Well I don't know, I mean, maybe yours are expensive or something. But . . . yeah, let's do that."

We both paused and then began unlacing, reaching down and groaning slightly. We unlaced in silence. Slowly. Not wanting to compete or confront in any way. Friendly. After we'd unlaced one shoe, I asked, "Should we do both?"

"Yeah, why not," he said.

It took a while, and the image of us side by side, unlacing our shoes—well, that took me back almost more than I could stand. Anyway it was over soon.

We relaced our shoes with the other's shoestrings and looked at each other and laughed.

After a moment he said, "Judy's good at this," thinking out loud.

"Yeah. Not bad," I said.

And then he said he was going to use the bathroom before he met his next guest. I nodded and we shook hands. Then I walked out into the hallway.

IN A NOSTALGIC, ultimately sad daze, I walked down the stairs to my next room. The third floor had gained some activity in my absence. People were talking softly outside doors. Some had already established roommates and were in their pajamas sipping from champagne glasses. The party was slowly evolving to the dual theme of nocturnal and nuptial.

I passed a few more gently speaking couples and triples and made my way to the end of the hallway. I was about to enter my room when the door suddenly opened and an agitated woman appeared holding what looked like a comic book about Taoism.

"Whew. You going in there?"

I nodded.

She giggled. "Good luck. A little creepy."

"Oh yeah?"

"And smelly. Oh it's not so bad," she said and glanced down at her book. "I'm sure you'll get something from it," she said, and walked away.

I entered and closed the door behind me. The room was dark and even the curtains had been drawn. Only a thin square of moonlight from the outline of the window managed to give the room's furniture some sense of depth and position.

"Come in. I'm on the bed over here. I hope you don't mind, but I like it dark."

"No, of course," I said.

I noticed the smell then. A rotting, diseased smell of putrefying shit and urine. Sweet, acrid, and nauseating all at once. I wanted to leave.

"Come sit down." I managed to find a corner of a bed and sat down guardedly, ready to make a break for the door. His voice had a strange, hollow quality, and I only had a dim idea of where he was in the room. This made me nervous.

"My name's Mac. What's yours?"

"Frank," I said.

"Hmph. That's interesting." Then there were a few minutes of silence as we contemplated each other's names.

I had been filled, while talking to Jim, with a bittersweet sadness. That he hadn't recognized me, that I was—and our mutual experiences were—unrecognizable to him filled me with a futile and complete sense of longing. And yet I knew it was incorrect to reach across to him with any act of familiarity. Yet now, in this darkened room with its penetrating odor and its hollow voice—I began to feel empty, emptied of all feeling, and the numbness, the void in my lungs and heart, started to scare me.

"If you feel across the bed, you'll find some books. Two left, should be."

I let my hand feel slowly across the bedspread, not knowing what snapping trap could be waiting. But there were just the books, like he said.

"Found them."

"Pick one," he said. "Either one, but I guess I'll need the other so don't take both. You can leave me something on the table by the door. Nice meeting you . . . Frank. Enjoy the book."

I got up slowly. I shoved my hands in my pockets to find something to leave but all I had were my keys. I pulled out my wallet but couldn't really see what I might leave. I just wanted to get out of there so took out a bill—I didn't even know what denomination—and placed it on the room's desk. "OK," I said, "I left something. It's not that interesting maybe, but it's all I have at the moment."

"No, I'm sure it's fine. I'll enjoy it."

"OK. Good night then and . . . good luck, Mac."

"Same to you, Frank."

I emerged into the light of the hallway shaken. I could still smell the putrid air of the room hanging on me and I went over to a window to get some fresh air. Looking at the book, I gathered it was an auto-repair manual.

My interaction with Mac had shaken me. The smell of death and sickness was oddly familiar and I thought Judy was giving me a Dickens trip—Ghosts of Christmas Past and Present, with me unwittingly playing Scrooge. As I made this association, I grew angry. Was Judy giving me some kind of moral lesson? I felt condescended to. But maybe her role was less creator than I assumed, and maybe I was as much an author of the night's events as she was. I made my way to the third room with some trepidation.

THE ROOM WAS on the first floor. The party was debauching itself rapidly now. Some civilized necking and lovers' talk in hallways, but passing doors revealed various polite to dangerous to athletic methods of fornication. Still in others, groups had either opted to skip or had finished, or were resting between such exertions and were now laughing, some arguing or crying, or, with blank expressions, watching television, or sleeping. I smiled. Judy, the architect, had rendered a living section of Marriage's house.

I made it to my last door and paused. I was nervous and scared but also wanted to enjoy my anticipation. How often are there rooms and doors with people behind those doors just—waiting for you. It's then a game, and the design, accounting for you, satisfies your ego and tells you that you're loved. I stepped into the room and laughed.

Jacob was there, dressed only in cotton pajama bottoms.

"How funny," he said, "I was just going to get dressed and see if you were waiting for me."

We approached each other wordlessly. I badly needed to fondle the Ghost of Christmas Future, to hump away the stink and memory of the previous two rooms. I got on my knees and gently eased down the cotton pants and stroked his cock to erection. Then he quickly undressed me and we kissed for a long time, then lay down head to feet, unthinking and sucking.

I came first. He then turned and positioned me on my hands and knees, asking me if it was OK. I nodded. He licked and fingered my asshole gently. When I was ready, he gave me a condom that I put on his cock. Then he fucked me.

While he did so, I thought of the countless times I'd done the same at Madeleine's brothel and I realized that I'm ruined for love not because I go and have paid anonymous mechanical sex every week but rather went there in the first place because I knew I was already ruined for it. That this act with Jacob, rare in its mutual desire, still has the familiar unshakable stench of ruin.

So as Jacob groans and comes and flops onto the bed next to me and as I smell my own shit smell and as I lie on his arm and we hold each other silently and as I'm pantomiming caresses of tenderness, I focus all my attention on these acts and perceptions so I will no longer bear witness to my own thoughts.

IN THE MORNING Jacob rises first and dresses. He tries to wake me several times but I just pretend to sleep. Finally he says, "The ceremony is starting soon. Do you want me to wait for you?" I can tell he's hurt by my not getting up, but I don't have the energy to face him. "Go on ahead. I'll be down soon," I say.

Eventually I dress and go down and manage to catch the tail end of the ceremony from the back. It's a beautiful morning and the bride and groom look correct and good. A real couple, I think. And: I hope it works out.

As a final Judy touch, the guests all leave before the bride and groom. We all line up and say our last farewells. When I get to the head of the line, Jim looks at me and says, "Look, Axel, I got married in your shoestrings." I look down and he displays the shoes and we laugh. "Congratulations," I say. Judy only says, "Thank you. Thank you for coming."

And as the guests leave one by one, as the cars pull out of the driveway, we are all left with the image of Jim and Judy remaining, waving good-bye. The people around them slowly diminishing until they can put down their tired arms, blink at the last car disappearing over the hill, and turn toward each other.

IN MY RENTAL, ON THE WAY BACK to the airport, I thought how impressive Judy was, how again she had defied my expectations. I briefly thought, then, that now a new possibility was being offered to me and I was, for a moment, optimistic, and felt cleansed and renewed.

But that day's hope turned out to be deceptive. When I think, now, of how I saw that wedding, as a promise of some change, of some beginning to some passionate and redeeming adventure, I can't help but cringe.

But I was right to be that way, I justify to myself after a moment. If I hadn't hoped *then,* well what would there have been to redeem?

But the truth is: nothing changed. The party faded and I went onward. The fact is, now I barely remember, or rather I barely ever have reason to remember, the wedding. And on those rare occasions when I do think of it, it is only in this way, like an embarrassing necessity, a lucky aberration zigzagging and which, thankfully, led to some, now distant and past, nadir.

CODA MERGE

Before turning down the sheets for bed, Cog called out
to his friend and spouse, Far:

"Dear would you
mind bringing me
cold water."

"Don't patronize me!
        you dung bag!"

was her fierce reply
though she did
bring a glass though
the fluid was tepid.

        Then
Far said Cog
I am pregnant
with our child.

Abort! said Far
said Cog
        Abort!
Abort!

To stop his blubbering Cog relented as much to say

Oh get under the sheets
I'll give to your sores.
Lie down.
            My hands
will give you a
      rub.

Far bit his lip so
he wouldn't become
too excited.

Acknowledgments

I finished writing *Fog & Car* on a bright afternoon in the summer of 2001. I remember rising from my desk in the small apartment we felt lucky to live in and walking two steps into the living room to tell a friend who was staying on our couch that I'd finished—but both of us, for different reasons, didn't quite seem to believe it. This was in a disheveled building situated between Carroll Gardens and Red Hook, and through the kitchen window you could see the Brooklyn-Queens Expressway nearly spitting distance away, floating on huge metal and concrete supports. When trucks ran over the seams of the BQE, the entire building rumbled. A few months later, through that same kitchen window, my roommates and I watched the second tower stream smoke and then fall. Much seemed to change immediately after, but I was a terrible futurist. I remember telling my friend Ning that cell phones would never take off—as who needed *even more* of the internet in their lives.

Many thanks to my agent, Marya Spence, for her wisdom and guidance, and to Chris Fischbach for supporting and acquiring this work. A Vulcan salute to Jeremy M. Davies. And much gratitude to the hardworking staff at Coffee House Press, with special thanks to Erika Stevens, Lizzie Davis, Mark Haber, Daley Farr, Abbie Phelps, Zoë Koenig, Quynh Van, and Laura Graveline.

Thank you to Jill Magi of sonaweb.net, and to the editors of elimae.com, in which portions of this book first appeared in slightly different forms. Thank you to Johannah Rodgers for encouraging me to publish it and for cofounding Ellipsis Press with me. Tremendous gratitude to Renee Gladman, Lynn Crawford, and Garielle Lutz. And a bow in remembrance for the late, brilliant writer Steve Katz.

Thank you and love to Shannon Steneck, Jamil Thomas, Corey Frost, Anelise Chen, Lisa Chen, Alex Samsky, Alan Davies, and Danny Tunick. A bow in Ning Li's direction, a subtle head nod to David McAleer, and a hug and wink to all the ghosts of youth that haunt 656 Henry.

Love always—along with a funny spray of marigolds, tulips, and ranunculus—for Joanna and Felix.

Coffee House Press began as a small letterpress operation in 1972 and has grown into an internationally renowned non-profit publisher of literary fiction, essay, poetry, and other work that doesn't fit neatly into genre categories.

Coffee House is both a publisher and an arts organization. Through our *Books in Action* program and publications, we've become interdisciplinary collaborators and incubators for new work and audience experiences. Our vision for the future is one where a publisher is a catalyst and connector.

LITERATURE
is not the same thing as
PUBLISHING

Funder Acknowledgments

Coffee House Press is an internationally renowned independent book publisher and arts nonprofit based in Minneapolis, MN; through its literary publications and *Books in Action* program, Coffee House acts as a catalyst and connector—between authors and readers, ideas and resources, creativity and community, inspiration and action.

Coffee House Press books are made possible through the generous support of grants and donations from corporations, state and federal grant programs, family foundations, and the many individuals who believe in the transformational power of literature. This activity is made possible by the voters of Minnesota through a Minnesota State Arts Board Operating Support grant, thanks to the legislative appropriation from the Arts and Cultural Heritage Fund. Coffee House also receives major operating support from the Amazon Literary Partnership, Jerome Foundation, Literary Arts Emergency Fund, McKnight Foundation, and the National Endowment for the Arts (NEA). To find out more about how NEA grants impact individuals and communities, visit www.arts.gov.

Coffee House Press receives additional support from Bookmobile; the Buckley Charitable Fund; Dorsey & Whitney LLP; the Gaea Foundation; the Schwab Charitable Fund; and the U.S. Bank Foundation.

The Publisher's Circle of Coffee House Press

Publisher's Circle members make significant contributions to Coffee House Press's annual giving campaign. Understanding that a strong financial base is necessary for the press to meet the challenges and opportunities that arise each year, this group plays a crucial part in the success of Coffee House's mission.

Recent Publisher's Circle members include many anonymous donors, Patricia A. Beithon, Theodore Cornwell, Jane Dalrymple-Hollo, Mary Ebert & Paul Stembler, Randy Hartten & Ron Lotz, Amy L. Hubbard & Geoffrey J. Kehoe Fund of the St. Paul & Minnesota Foundation, Hyde Family Charitable Fund, Cinda Kornblum, Gillian McCain, Mary & Malcolm McDermid, Vance Opperman, Mr. Pancks' Fund in memory of Graham Kimpton, Robin Preble, Steve Smith, and Paul Thissen.

For more information about the
Publisher's Circle and other ways to support
Coffee House Press books, authors, and activities, please visit
www.coffeehousepress.org/pages/support-coffee-house
or contact us at info@coffeehousepress.org.

COFFEE HOUSE PRESS began as a small letterpress operation in 1972. In the years since, it has grown into an internationally renowned nonprofit publisher of literary fiction, nonfiction, poetry, and other writing that doesn't fit neatly into genre categories. Our mission is to expand definitions of what literature can be, what it can do, and to whom it belongs.

FURTHER FICTION TITLES FROM COFFEE HOUSE PRESS

Cecilia $14.95
K-MING CHANG

We're Safe When We're Alone . $14.95
NGHIEM TRAN

The Devil of the Provinces . . $17.95
JUAN CÁRDENAS (TRANSLATED BY LIZZIE DAVIS)

The Plotinus $14.95
RIKKI DUCORNET

When the Hibiscus Falls $17.95
M. EVELINA GALANG

The Nature Book $16.95
TOM COMITTA

Jawbone $16.95
MÓNICA OJEDA (TRANSLATED BY SARAH BOOKER)

Saint Sebastian's Abyss . . . $16.95
MARK HABER

Till the Wheels Fall Off $17.95
BRAD ZELLAR

Temporary $16.95
HILARY LEICHTER

One Night Two Souls Went Walking $16.95
ELLEN COONEY

trans(re)lating house one . . $17.95
POUPEH MISSAGHI

I Hotel $21.95
KAREN TEI YAMASHITA

Last Days $16.95
BRIAN EVENSON

Fish in Exile $16.95
VI KHI NAO

The Story of My Teeth $16.95
VALERIA LUISELLI (TRANSLATED BY CHRISTINA MACSWEENEY)

Leaving the Atocha Station $18
BEN LERNER

The Pink Institution $16.95
SELAH SATERSTROM

For more information about Coffee House Press and how you can support our mission, please visit coffeehousepress.org/pages/support-coffee-house

Professors may request desk copies by visiting coffeehousepress.org/pages/educators